6-22-13

With best regards

Thank you!

Millie Curtis

The Newcomer

by

Millie Curtis

Avid Readers Publishing Group
Lakewood, California

Acknowledgements

My heartfelt thanks to the following people who contributed their talents to this novel:

Elizabeth Blye: photographer, computer guru and fixer of a myriad of problems.

Katherine Cobb: cover design.

Anica Moran: my lovely and willing model.

Bonnie Carter, Catherine Owens, Jean Malucci and Fred Curtis: eagle eye proofreaders.

BJ Applegren, Tara Bell, Katherine Cobb and Karen Robbins: all writers in their own right, and the helpful writing group that kept me on track.

As always, thank you dear readers for allowing me to become a part of your life, if only for a little while.

This book is dedicated to the memory of my lovely sister, Amelia Ann Murray.
Meadie, the memories are priceless.

Chapter 1

Elizabeth Fairchilds, much to her dislike of having to do everything for herself, stacked logs and kindling on the back porch of her hat shop.

At age twenty, she had run this millinery for four months and disliked it so much she dreaded seeing another day approach.

Because her young world had turned topsy-turvy, her parents made the decision to buy the shop for her. Perhaps they thought they were doing what was best, but she would rather they had been more understanding about the circumstances that changed her life.

The parting words of her self-righteous mother still stung, "You have shamed us, Elizabeth. A change will do you good."

Her father had been empathetic. "A change will give you a new start, Lizzy."

Lizzy, a pet nickname usually uttered out of hearing distance of her mother or the retort would be, "Francis, her name is Elizabeth. If you wanted to call her Lizzy, you should have named her Lizzy!" Her father's reaction would be a sly smile and wink toward his daughter. As Elizabeth recalled this unspoken special bond they shared, it gave her a warm feeling.

When the Fairchilds bought this shop in Berryville for their daughter, they left a small sum of money in the local bank in Elizabeth's name to help with the transition. Of course the deed remained in their names, which meant she was still under their thumb.

But, the bank account was hers, her hope for tomorrow, a chance to get away from this small Virginia town and back to the city. How she missed the daily life of Washington, D.C., seventy miles east.

Not only would money in the bank free her from the confines of the town, it would also allow her to fulfill a mission that consumed her thoughts both day and night.

Growing the bank account was the reason Elizabeth was stacking the wood without help on this unseasonably cool day. She had paid a man to split the wood and he would have carried it to the porch for more money. But money was important to Elizabeth, so she chose to make trips of lugging the firewood from the backyard to the porch. A man could carry three times the load she struggled under. It was tiring work. Would she have enough for the winter? What did she know about stacking wood and keeping fireplaces going? Irritation peaked causing her to throw the last log with such force that it sailed over the railing. She shrugged her shoulders and stomped into the back room of the hat shop.

Elizabeth had spent one week under the tutelage of the previous owner, Catherine Burke, to learn how to run the millinery. One week wasn't enough. The private school Elizabeth had attended in Washington was no preparation for what faced her as a young woman on her own. What were her parents thinking to set her adrift in this place?

She dusted off her gloves and reset a hairpin into long blond curls before donning a white apron over a simple, blue, long-sleeved cotton dress. The toes of her laced, brown leather shoes were smudged with dirt. Elizabeth grabbed a tea towel off the table that sat in the middle of the back room and rubbed off the signs of her backyard labor. Skirt hems were rising because of the war in Europe; otherwise she wouldn't have to pay so much attention to her shoes. Although, from what she'd observed, it seemed the women in Berryville were not up to the styles of 1916.

The hat shop sat four steps up from the main street. Two identical sets of stairs and stoops led to her apartment on the west and the millinery shop on the east. A second-story, covered, wooden porch sheltered them both. The door to her living area opened into a comfortable foyer with a wide staircase leading up to Elizabeth's apartment. Back stairs led to the rear of the millinery.

The hat shop was long and narrow, dimly lit by light bulbs suspended from long cords hanging from the high ceiling. The bulbs were protected by glass shades. A display window in the front allowed shadowed light from the street. A small east window brought in the morning sun. Elizabeth had stationed a three-way mirror to catch as much light as possible for ladies to have a better view of hats they were considering.

The poorly lighted room seemed to match her dismal mood. The back room of the shop had a windowed wall that faced south. It was warm and cheery there and she spent as much of her time in that spot as she could. A few weeks ago, a man came by to see if the wall could be removed to allow more light to enter the main room of the shop. "No ma'am. That there's a weight bearin' wall. You'd end up with yer kitchen in the middle of the room." When that idea fell through, Elizabeth thought of contending with the dim areas of the shop by placing oil lamps. Perhaps that would help to lighten the room. Oil lamps would have to wait until she had money ahead to purchase them.

The early September day left a chill in the room. Elizabeth stoked the half-burned log in the fireplace before turning to the counter that held the day's work. There were hats in different stages of completion laying about the six-foot workspace. The task held no interest. In fact, Elizabeth had no interest in much of anything. How could her parents have had no qualms about dumping her in a place where she knew no one, and buy her a business she knew nothing about? Those thoughts brought tears to her eyes but she refused to cry. She had shed enough tears when she arrived in this static place where everything was foreign to her. If it hadn't been for sweet Mary Lee Thompson helping her in the shop, Elizabeth wasn't sure she would have survived this long.

The more she thought about her position, the more dejected she became. She had tried to put the unpleasantness out of her thoughts but that was impossible. As she sat and mulled over her unhappiness, realization struck her with a jolt so sudden she drew in her breath. It was an awakening! Like a slap in the face, it brought her to her senses. No one could solve her dilemma but herself. She could either wallow about in self-pity or she could grab the helm of the wheel and change her course. The passion of the moment was a sudden push and caused her to steel herself with the promise, "I will find him no matter what it takes."

How could she have been so blind? With renewed spirit she determined to forge ahead. There was purpose in this life and she had better get on with it.

****

Later in the morning, Mary Lee Thompson came by to help. Red hair peeked out from under her bonnet and framed her round face. The crisp air of the day gave her a rosy glow. She stretched up to hang her shawl on a peg behind the work counter. "My goodness, Miz' Elizabeth, I don't think you done too much since I was here last. You'll be surprised how many ladies will be lookin' for a new hat for when it turns cold. An' the holidays are comin' in December. Miz' Catherine made sure she had plenty of hats to choose from."

"I'm not the dedicated milliner that Mrs. Burke was," came Elizabeth's curt reply causing her chagrin that her retort had slipped out so easily. "I'm sorry, Mary Lee, that was unkind of me."

5

"But, that's okay, Miz' Elizabeth, if that's rightly how you feel, ain't it? What made you buy this shop, anyway?"

Elizabeth shifted uneasily in her chair. "I didn't buy it. My parents did. It's a long story and some day I will tell you."

That seemed to satisfy Mary Lee because she picked up an unfinished hat, "We'd best get started or there won't be many to sell."

"I know you're right. I just haven't put my heart into this business. I don't have the talent your Miss Catherine had. For the life of me, I can't think why she had such a difficult time selling this place. Especially since she was going to live in the city."

Mary Lee gathered three hats in front of her as she sat at the work counter facing Elizabeth. "You got to look at it this way. Yer a newcomer. Pretty soon you'll git used to this place an' townfolks'll git used to you. Miz' Catherine was born and raised here an' that makes a difference. I did get a nice card from her. She's all set up in her shop in Georgetown an' has more orders than she can keep up with. She wanted me to come and work with her, but..." A big smile lit up her cheery face. "I met a man whose been hired to run a big farm down south of town." With a sideways look she continued, "I like him right fine. Besides, Berryville is all I know an' I'd never leave here."

Elizabeth had to smile. Mary Lee was always so perky it was difficult to stay in a disgruntled mood. "Why don't I go fix a nice cup of tea and you can tell me all about this man you've met. I could use some good news."

Mary Lee looked at her across the work counter. "If you don't mind my askin', Miz' Elizabeth, how old are you?"

"I don't mind. Two weeks ago I turned twenty."

"An' you never said a word. Yer too young to be unhappy all the time."

"How do you know that I'm not happy?"

"Wal', I prob'ly shouldn't say this, but I can see it in yer eyes, an' the way you walk, an' talk an' how you pretty much keep to yerself. I went through some hard times an' I know what it's like to be sad. Did you lose somebody?"

Elizabeth leaned back in her chair and looked wistfully at the young lady across from her. "You could say that. How old are you, Mary Lee?"

"I just turned twenty-one."

"Then I guess because you're a widow and a year older that makes you wiser. I have decided to get a brighter outlook and maybe you can help me."

Mary Lee's round blue eyes opened wide. "However do you 'spect me to do that?" she asked with alarm.

"Having you around is good for me. I am going to brew some tea and see if we can get warmed up. Would you like to have me read your tealeaves when we are done?"

The willing helper dropped the hat she was working on. "You can do that?"

"Yes I can and I'm good at it." Elizabeth knew from experience. When she was in finishing school, all the girls wanted her to read their tealeaves because much of what she predicted came true.

Mary Lee was skeptical. "I don't want you to tell me nothin' bad. I've had enough of that already."

"I promise to tell you nothing but the good things I see."

"Can you read yer own fortune in the leaves?"

Elizabeth shook her head with a lofty air. "A tealeaves reader never reads her own." Although, she had made that mistake once and the leaves were right. They brought her grief.

Mary Lee was always inspired when it came to hearing about fortune telling. She leaned forward in earnest. "How did you learn it? I mean, how do you know how to read leaves? They don't look like anythin' to me."

Elizabeth gave a cheery smile. "I had a wonderful grandmother who taught me when I was nine years old. I'd go over to her house on Sunday afternoons after church. We'd sit and have a cup of tea and sour cream cookies. She made the best sour cream cookies." The thought gave a tug at her heart. "After we finished our tea, she would read the leaves and show me what they meant."

Mary Lee was captivated. "You were so lucky, Miz' Elizabeth. My grandma wasn't good fer much; she would jus' rock in her rocker all day and try to hit us with her cane if we came near."

Elizabeth couldn't imagine it. "That's dreadful! Was she always like that?"

"Long as I 'member. She died when I was ten. My mama cried, but I didn't feel bad about it."

"My grandmother died when I was twelve and I thought my world had come to an end. I think she was the only one in the world who truly loved me."

Mary Lee paused, "You know, Miz' Elizabeth, we've never talked like this before an' I think we need that tea 'cuz I'm beginin' to feel pretty sad myself."

Elizabeth pushed away from the cluttered work area. "You are right. We don't need to be sitting here and feeling melancholy. You get back to those hats while I put the kettle over."

"What's that big word mean you just said?"

"Melancholy? It means being unhappy or down-in-the-dumps."

Mary Lee laughed. "Miz' Catherine was always sayin' them big words. I guess you went all through school like she did."

"Where I went, they called it finishing school. We not only learned reading, writing, and arithmetic, we learned proper etiquette. I know the proper way to pour tea and what fork to use with a salad and…"

"An' lotsa big words," Mary Lee chimed in and shook her head. "You make me laugh, Miz' Elizabeth. I guess you feel better."

9

"That I do, Mary Lee. That I do."

Elizabeth went to make the tea. When she returned, Mary Lee had put another log on the fire. "Thank you for tending the fireplace. I forgot the fire was getting low. I should have remembered."

"They most likely didn't teach that in the school where you went. Miz' Elizabeth, you need to get out of this shop. Robert is goin' to pick me up on Sunday to show me the farm where he works. Would you like to go with us?"

Elizabeth sipped tea before she answered. The thought of getting out of town and her apartment was appealing. She'd been cooped up in this place since she'd arrived. Still, she was cautious with her reply, "I'm not sure your young man would be pleased to have another person along. It would be an imposition on my part."

"There you go with one of them big words agin'. If it means you think yer goin' to be in the way that ain't true. I wouldn't ask if I thought it would upset Robert."

Elizabeth didn't give an answer. Instead, she said, "Tell me about this new man in your life."

Mary Lee stopped working and picked up her teacup. She wiggled her small frame into the chair to get more comfortable. "Robert's a speck older than me. He's got hair the color of copper and freckles like me and he's not real tall." Then she quickly added, "But he's mighty strong."

"Where did you meet him?"

"I met him at the cinema. I was sittin' there by myself and he was sittin' next to me by hisself an' we just got to talkin'."

"Oh, Mary Lee, that sounds risky, but also exciting."

"Miz' Elizabeth, I'm not one to go aroun' talkin' to strange men, an' I think I learned, after bein' married to Zack, what to watch out for in men." She shook her head. "Zack was no account right from the start. He drank too much and was drunk when he got run over by the train."

"Why did you marry him?"

"I don' know. "I guess it's 'cause I was young, an' he was good lookin', and everybody 'round here thinks a girl ought to get married by the time she's fifteen."

Elizabeth gave a wistful look. "Where I come from, it's eighteen. One goes to finishing school and then finds a man of substance and breeding."

"Is that what happened to you, Miz' Elizabeth?"

"As I said before, it's a long story."

Mary Lee quickly changed the subject. "Robert's a happy and kind person, an' you still haven't tol' me whether you want to go with us on Sunday afternoon. He's right proud of the farm where he works so he'll be pleased to show it to both of us."

"Then if you're that sure, I'll be happy to go."

Mary Lee was excited. "I can hardly wait. Robert said he can borrow the carriage on Sunday so we can ride in style."

Elizabeth had to smile. Was there any other way to travel?

"I'd like to have you call me Elizabeth. We're friends and that's what friends do."

"Yeah, but you an' me are different. I mean, you didn't grow up here an' all an' you've done seen more than I have, an' you do own the shop, an'…"

Elizabeth interrupted, "Well, for heaven's sake, if it's that difficult forget I asked."

"Okay," Mary Lee chirped.

Sunday was going to be an adventure. The dreariness of the morning washed away.

Chapter 2

Sunday turned out to be a beautiful Indian summer day. Elizabeth waited in the foyer at the foot of the stairs. She wanted to wait on the stoop to soak up the warmth of the day, but she didn't care to have anyone see her standing there, certainly not that nosy editor's wife, Lavinia Talley, who lived catty-corner across the street. Her husband owned and edited the Clarke Courier, a weekly newspaper filled with all the latest social news of the county. Elizabeth had done her best to discourage Lavinia from the time they first met because Catherine, the former milliner, had warned of Lavinia's tendency to spread tales. 'She means well, but it would be wise to be on guard. The story is never the same once she has peddled what she considers to be news.' Elizabeth had heeded Catherine's words. One learns quickly when one has been the target of gossip.

It was close to eleven o'clock when Elizabeth saw a shiny, black carriage pull up across the street in front of the bank. Mary Lee was sitting on the front bench next to the driver, whom Elizabeth assumed was Robert. Before he could alight, Elizabeth was out the door and down the four steps to the sidewalk and crossing the street in a hurry.

The driver stepped out of the carriage to meet her. Mary Lee called from her seat in the carriage, "Miz' Elizabeth, this is Robert Graves. Robert, Miz' Elizabeth Fairchilds."

"I'm right proud to meet you ma'am," he said as he removed his cap in a shy manner.

"As I am to meet you, Robert. I'm pleased that Mary Lee invited me to come along, but I don't care to be in the way."

"No ma'am. It will be nice to have you with us."

Out of the corner of her eye, Elizabeth saw the lace curtains in Lavinia's window move, as though touched by a wisp of air. Robert offered his arm to help Elizabeth into the stately carriage that was covered by a black leather top.

She was tastefully dressed in an embroidered white, high collared, long sleeved blouse, and a navy blue skirt that came to mid-calf. A delicate organza scarf draped over a large straw hat was tied under her chin. How she wished she could have worn one of the fashionable double-skirted outfits she had brought from Washington, but Elizabeth knew that Mary Lee would be wearing a simple outfit, and it wouldn't be right to out-dress the person who had invited her.

Robert was as Mary Lee had described and they made a pleasing couple. His cordial, easy manner dispelled any reservations Elizabeth had as she settled comfortably next to Mary Lee.

They rode out of town on Church Street to the main pike. Twenty minutes later Robert made a left turn onto a dirt lane. When they crested a small hill, the country scene opened up. In the distance to her right, sat a large limestone house atop a small rise with a background of trees in full fall colors and the aptly named Blue Ridge Mountains behind.

"Oh, Mary Lee. Have you ever seen anything so beautiful?" Elizabeth exclaimed.

"I do declare. It is the prettiest I've ever seen," Mary Lee answered.

Robert Graves grinned from ear to ear. He stopped at a limestone cottage to the left that sat a few feet from the lane.

"This is my place," he informed them. "Would you ladies like to stop and have a cool drink of water? We have the best tasting spring water around."

"What do you think, Miz' Elizabeth?" Mary Lee asked. "I know I could use a drink."

"I can't turn down your offer, Robert," Elizabeth replied.

Besides, it would give the young ladies a chance to get inside and see how a bachelor lives. He pulled the horse to a stop in front of the cottage and then helped the ladies down. The hem on Mary Lee's dress got pinched between the step and the carriage. "Oh my good gracious, I cain't move or I'm gonna' tear my dress right off!"

Her face turned beet red and both Elizabeth and Robert were quick to rush to her aid. It took a few minutes for them to wrest the squeezed material without damaging the lace. All three were laughing at the gyrations they went through to unbind it. Elizabeth helped Mary Lee smooth both her dress, and her embarrassment, before they happily continued into the house, where they found it neat and tidy.

It was definitely a man's abode. A shotgun hung above a stone fireplace. The room was both a living area and kitchen. A stuffed chair with scruffy plaid cushions sat in a corner and a plain round oak table with three chairs took up the middle of the room. There were no vases of flowers or fancy dishes or frilly curtains. Elizabeth and Mary Lee took a seat at the table while Robert pumped water and brought them each a cold drink in pottery mugs.

There was an awkward silence until Mary Lee broke it with saying, "Robert, yer place is comfortable."

"It is that," agreed Elizabeth, although she couldn't imagine living in it.

"I brought us a picnic basket of lunch," offered Mary Lee. "Is there a pretty place for us to spread a blanket?"

Robert seemed relieved at the thought of being on the move. "Once you ladies are ready, I'd like to show you the stables, and then a perfect spot where we can eat."

Elizabeth was apologetic. "Mary Lee, it was good of you to pack a lunch. I never thought to ask if I could bring anything. All I brought was my shawl and a book to read."

Admiration was evident as Mary Lee gave a warm smile to Robert before she addressed Elizabeth. "When Robert asked me to come, I told him I would pack a lunch. It was no trouble to pack fer three people as well as two."

"Well, I'm not going to turn down some good food, and I am dying to see the stables," Elizabeth confessed.

Robert picked up their mugs and placed them in a small sink. "Let's be on our way."

Back in the carriage, they followed the dirt lane around a couple of curves until they came to the stables. Here, there was a commanding view of the mountains. The meadows were bereft of trees, and livestock had closely cropped the grass of the fields. The carriage stopped in front of a long, whitewashed, one story building. Horses' heads poked out over the open half doors in the stalls.

"We'll go inside. I have some handsome colts I want you to see," said the proud Robert.

Elizabeth walked behind to let Robert and Mary Lee have some time together. She patted the faces of the inquisitive horses that came to the front of their stalls. It had been a few years since she had been this close to a horse. Riding lessons were insisted upon when she was growing up.

Robert and Mary Lee were standing at a small corral and viewing three smart-looking colts, where he was explaining the important points one looks for when judging a horse's value. Mary Lee was intent. Elizabeth was indifferent. She politely voiced her admiration for the colts before she decided it was the perfect opportunity to leave the couple by themselves. "I spied a lovely large oak tree on that rise over to the right of the stables. Do you mind if I go to sit under the oak to read a bit of my book before we enjoy our picnic?"

They turned their attention to Elizabeth.

"We don't mind, Miz' Elizabeth. The blanket is sittin' on top of the picnic basket in the back of the carriage. Would you like fer me to get it?" asked Mary Lee.

"No, thank you. I'll pick it up on my way by. You two come along whenever you're ready to eat."

"You don't mind goin' by yerself? We can walk you up."

"Not a bit," answered Elizabeth. "I'll be in plain sight."

She left and was walking towards the carriage when she stopped to watch four mounted riders come thundering past her on their way to the stables.

After she waved away the dust they had stirred up, she took her handbag containing a book and shawl from the carriage. These she carried, along with the blanket, up a steep grassy knoll to sit under the shade of the majestic tree. It was a quiet and restful spot to either read or let her mind wander as she surveyed the countryside.

****

Andrew Caldwell, one of the four riders, was hot and thirsty after the long morning ride. His hat, breeches and shirt were wet with sweat. He removed his cap and wiped his auburn hair with a handkerchief he wore around his neck.

"Come in and have some refreshments," offered a fellow rider.

"Thank you, Charles, but I have to get back to Washington. With this war in Europe going on, I hate to take any time away. The ride was what I needed. I'll get a drink from the well and be on my way."

"Are we going to be dragged into that war?"

"I certainly hope not," answered Andrew.

His friend smiled as he patted him on the shoulder. "Glad you could come with us. Take care of yourself."

Andrew walked to the well and drew up a bucket of water. Taking an enamel cup from a hook, he dipped it into the bucket and savored a long cool drink. He sloshed a handkerchief in the cool water and wiped his face. He was in a pensive mood. Andrew had done a lot of thinking lately. At twenty-five, he wasn't that pleased with his life. It wasn't because of money or women, both were plentiful. And, it wouldn't be long before he moved up in rank in the army. What more he was looking for he wasn't sure. The feeling that something was missing in his life started with a stint of filling in for his fellow captain, Asa Thomas. Asa's baby daughter arrived while he was on assignment in England, so Andrew stepped in to help his wife, Carolyn, until the new father returned. It was an unaccustomed role but one Andrew found he enjoyed.

Leaning against the well while looking over the Mitchell estate, he spied Elizabeth, at a distance, sitting under the tree. It was in the direction he was going. Perhaps he would just stop by and introduce himself. Andrew was never shy when it came to a young lady. His horse had been watered and rested and ready for the final ride home. He tied his jacket behind his saddle, placed his cap on his head and started out. He left his horse to graze before walking up the hill to where Elizabeth was sitting.

A light shawl covered her lap. Apparently, she had become so absorbed in the book she was reading she didn't hear the rustle of leaves as Andrew approached.

"Good afternoon," he said, tipping his cap.

She let out a cry of surprise causing the book to slip from her hands. She had removed her shoes so she quickly pulled the shawl lower to cover the lisle stockings peeking out from beneath her skirt.

"I'm sorry. I didn't mean to startle you. You looked so peaceful up here that I had to stop and introduce myself. I'm Andrew Caldwell."

"Elizabeth Fairchilds," she replied, without a smile or an offer of her hand. "You were one of the riders I saw going to the stables?" she asked.

"Yes. We had a vigorous ride and now I'm on my way home."

"You're not taking the main road?"

He laughed, sending crinkles around his green eyes. "No, it's shorter to cut across the fields." He dropped his lithe six-foot frame onto the grass and sat Indian style.

Elizabeth hadn't moved. She sat upright, her hands clutching the book she'd reclaimed.

He plucked a long blade of grass and chewed on the end of it before he spoke. "Are you visiting?"

"I live in town."

"You must be new to Clarke County. I thought I knew all the pretty young ladies in these parts. Have you lived here long?"

"Long enough," she remarked, as she found a page in the book and began to read.

It was not the way the handsome Andrew was used to being received. He sat for a moment and studied her as she read. Or was she pretending?

It was an awkward silence between them until he said, "Well, I see Robert and his friend heading this way with a basket. It's a beautiful day for a picnic."

She didn't invite him to stay.

He tipped his cap once more. "Miss Fairchilds, I'll be on my way. Perhaps we will meet again."

"Perhaps we will."

He whistled to his horse that came at his command. Without a word he bolted up into the saddle and was off. Elizabeth raised her eyes from the page and watched as he galloped across the open field.

Mary Lee waved to her on their way up the hill.

"Was that Captain Caldwell ridin' away?" Robert asked.

"I don't know if he's a captain or not. He introduced himself as Andrew Caldwell."

"His folks have a big place over yonder. He's quite the ladies' man, so I'm told." Robert grinned.

"I can understand why," Elizabeth said, "but I don't think he looked at this lady as a conquest."

Robert offered a wary eye. "From what I hear, ladies take to the Captain like hens take to corn."

Mary Lee, apparently uncomfortable with the trend of the conversation, piped in, "I'm right starved. I brought fried chicken, biscuits and salad."

Elizabeth smiled. "It sounds delicious and I could eat a whole chicken. How about you, Robert?"

"You're right about that, Miz' Elizabeth. We might have to fight over the chicken."

Mary Lee gave a relieved chuckle. "Be sure and leave room for apple pie. I found the nicest early apples, and I couldn't help but put them in a big pie."

The three ate their lunch and made small talk as if they had shared many lovely afternoon picnics together.

It was close to four o'clock when they started for Berryville. Elizabeth had enjoyed the day, and loathed the idea of going back to her lonely apartment where her mind would wrestle with the problem that lay ahead of her.

She did have a plan, which would take courage and money. She had become a good steward of her finances, but the hat shop was just breaking even. It was clear she would have to make it profitable if she were going to raise the money she needed. Time was not on her side.

Chapter 3

The next week proved to be a flurry of activity. Mary Lee had said there would be a big Harvest Party at the end of October and ladies would be looking for hats and gloves. Elizabeth ordered with caution because she was reluctant to use money out of her bank account.

On Monday, a traveling salesman had come by the shop.

"You ought to think about carrying this jewelry. It's a new line that our company has started to provide."

He showed Elizabeth stickpins, bracelets, broaches, hatpins, earrings and necklaces. Elizabeth was awed by the display of cameos, porcelain, glass-beads, and pearls. Every color, shape and style dazzled before her eyes. Yet... she hesitated.

"There's a jeweler in town. I'm not sure there would be enough business for me to invest in this."

"The jeweler sells the good stuff," the salesman rationalized. "This is fun stuff that ladies want to wear."

"I wouldn't care to have the jeweler think I was competing with him."

The little round man picked up a bead necklace and dangled it on his fingertips. "No ma'am, he'd just look at this and snicker."

"But I have to be careful about what I put my money into. I don't want to lose this shop."

"Just try a few pieces and see how they sell. I can tell you they are all the rage in the city. You'd be the first one around here to offer them."

Elizabeth sat back in her chair and fingered her blond curls. She looked at the lovely display of jewelry spread across the counter. If she could match jewelry with hats and fashions, perhaps it would work. Mary Lee had said the two big selling times coming up were the Harvest Party and Christmas. Giving it much thought, Elizabeth decided that now would be the best time to try.

The salesman was eager to help her with what he considered good buys, and Elizabeth had an eye for fashion so between them they picked out a variety of pieces. The pleased salesman left the shop with an order of one hundred dollars and a big smile on his face.

Elizabeth watched him leave and hoped she had done the right thing. It was half the money she had in the bank. The jewelry would either put more funds in her account or put the shop in danger of going under. Well, it was done and she wasn't going to worry about it.

On Friday, Mary Lee stopped to see if she could help. "I swear, Miz' Elizabeth, I've been so busy this week I ain't been able to get by. From the looks of it, you've been right busy."

25

"I'm trying. Do you like the way I've moved the furniture around? I think the shop looks better. I haven't moved the work counter yet because it's too heavy." She pointed to the side of the room. "I want to put it the long way. Do you think we can move it together?"

"I'm not rightly sure. Neither one of us is very big and these oak pieces are mighty heavy." Mary Lee paused, as if thinking whether it was possible. "Ya' know, Miz' Elizabeth, why don't we wait until this evenin'. Robert is comin' in to take me to the cinema. He wouldn't mind helpin'."

Elizabeth didn't even have to think about it. "That sounds like the best idea yet. I'll put the kettle on for tea while you gather up what we need to work on."

"And, I want you to read my tealeaves today," Mary Lee called after her.

When Elizabeth returned, she took her seat opposite her friend. "I enjoyed our picnic last Sunday. Robert seems like a nice person. I think you were lucky to meet him."

A grin spread across Mary Lee's face as she blushed. "He's the nicest man I've ever met. He liked you. He said he was afraid you were goin' to be uppity like some of them women from Washington."

"How did he know I was from Washington? Did you tell him?"

"No, it wasn't me. But you know how it is 'round here. Word gets out whether you want it to or not."

"Speaking of word getting out, look who's waddling across the street."

"Oh, no, don't tell me it's Miz' Talley."

"She probably saw you come in and is going to ask you about Robert. I'm sure that word is out."

"I'm gonna hide," Mary Lee said.

"Too late," Elizabeth smiled.

The bell jingled as Lavinia made her entrance. "Good morning, girls. It's a bit chilly out there."

"May I help you, Mrs. Talley?" asked Elizabeth.

"No thank you, my dear. I came over to ask if you would like to attend the church supper at Grace Episcopal on Sunday. You can come, too, Mary Lee, although you don't go to our church."

Mary Lee's grimace was hidden from Lavinia.

"That's kind of you to ask, but I have plans," Elizabeth said.

"Perhaps some other time," came the busybody's reply. "Mary Lee, I hear you've been keeping company with the new man the Mitchells hired."

"Yes ma'am," Mary Lee acknowledged.

"After the life you had with Zack, you had better be cautious."

"Yes ma'am." Mary Lee stabbed a needle into a pincushion.

"Well, I have to be on my way to see Irene Butler. It was nice to talk with you girls. If you change your mind, Elizabeth, let me know."

As soon as Lavinia was out the door, Mary Lee said, "That old biddy hen has to put her nose in everybody's business."

"She doesn't have anything else to do," Elizabeth responded. "It's kind of sad in a way."

"I don't feel bad fer her, an' I hear the pot whistlin'".

"You sound a bit vexed, Mary Lee," Elizabeth teased.

"That woman does that to me. She used to bother Miz' Catherine all the time when she owned the shop."

"Well, let's have our tea and improve our dispositions."

"Whatever that word means."

Elizabeth laughed as she left to prepare the tea. Rather than to put the leaves into the pot, she spooned them into their cups. The two sipped their tea until there were only a few drops of liquid left. Then Elizabeth instructed Mary Lee to swirl her cup around three times to let the leaves settle where they may. Mary Lee did as she was told. Elizabeth took the cup, being careful to hold it still. Then she peered into the flowered china cup keeping it almost at eye level.

Mary Lee leaned as far forward as possible on the work counter without leaving her chair. "What's it say, Miz' Elizabeth?"

"You have to give me a minute. We can't hurry the leaves."

"I hope you see somethin' good."

After a few seconds, Elizabeth held the cup so they could both look into it. "Look here, Mary Lee," Elizabeth said, tilting the cup toward her friend. "I see a ring. It's not a big ring and there are no stones, more like a band."

"Oh my Lord! You mean like a weddin' ring?"

"I can't say for sure that it's a wedding ring, but it's a ring. And, look over here. I see a big tree next to a small house. Do you have a tree next to your house?"

"There was a tree but it was cut down."

"This one isn't cut down. This one is a large tree, a beautiful tree."

Mary Lee's blue-eyes widened. "Remember when we went to where Robert lives? He had that big magnolia tree by his little house. We both said that we'd never seen one so big and the leaves were shinin' and dancin' in the sun."

Elizabeth answered, "I do remember that."

Mary Lee snatched the cup from Elizabeth's hands, "Don't be readin' no more, Miz' Elizabeth. You're beginnin' to make me think too much."

"I don't see anything else in there that has meaning."

"Good. I'm not wantin' to hear anymore. We need to git workin' on these hats 'cause the ladies will be comin' in next week to shop for the Harvest Party."

29

"Harvest Party? What's that about?"

"I'm not rightly sure. I guess it means that all the crops are in, an' all the people with means get all gussied up an' have a big party before winter sets in."

"That sounds perfect. The jewelry I ordered should be in by next week. It will give me a chance to see if it will sell."

"Jewelry?" Mary Lee asked, raising her eyebrows. "Maybe that's the ring you saw in my cup."

Elizabeth gave a wry smile. "That's possible." But Elizabeth knew that wasn't the ring she saw in the leaves.

Chapter 4

The next week in October brought the "uppity harvest ladies" as Mary Lee liked to refer to them. They were from the southern end of the county, where Elizabeth was told, ten percent of the people owned ninety percent of the land.

The jewelry had arrived as the salesman had promised. Elizabeth didn't have a display case so she piled up some boxes at different levels on the end of her work counter and draped them with a white cloth. Special care was taken to arrange each detailed piece, and when she was done she was pleased with the effort.

Mary Lee's response when she entered was rewarding to hear. "Miz' Elizabeth, I ain't never seen anythin' so pretty."

"Which one do you like best?"

Mary Lee took some time with her decision. "They're all so pretty it's hard to say, but I'm right partial to this cherry colored pin. The one shaped like a bow and has this little pearl danglin' down." She picked up the pin to admire it. "That would look right nice for Christmas."

"That it would," Elizabeth agreed. That evening, after Mary Lee left the shop, Elizabeth placed the pin back in its box and took it up to her apartment. It would make a perfect Christmas present for her friend.

****

Wednesday was her most profitable day. It was also the day she met Ruth Caldwell. When she entered the shop, Mary Lee retreated to the back room. Elizabeth was puzzled over her helper's reaction but went forward to greet her customer.

"Good afternoon," said Elizabeth.

Ruth ignored the greeting. "I haven't been here since Catherine owned the shop. She used to make an original design for me for the Harvest Party. I doubt you will be able to satisfy what I need."

Elizabeth wanted to tell the saucy woman that she had waited a bit late to get an original design, but held her tongue.

"I'll be happy to show you what I have on hand," Elizabeth replied. "Perhaps you would like to look over the jewelry that just arrived while I collect some hats."

Elizabeth didn't wait for a reply, and went to the back room of the shop. She whispered to Mary Lee, "Do you know this young lady and what she likes?"

Mary Lee whispered back, "Her name's Ruth Caldwell. She likes anythin' like what the ladies in Washington are wearin' and its got to be eye catchin'. Miz' Caldwell likes to be noticed."

"See if there is one of those unclaimed hats in the storage closet that you can fancy up. You're good at that." She didn't wait for Mary Lee's reaction.

Back in the shop, Elizabeth stalled for time. As she hoped, Ruth was fascinated by the jewelry.

Elizabeth fastened necklaces, clasped bracelets and dangled earrings until her saucy customer was satisfied. Not only did Ruth Caldwell leave with a fancy hat and gloves, she also bought the most expensive necklace with matching bracelet and earrings.

After she left, Mary Lee came to the front of the shop looking sheepish. "I'm sorry, Miz' Elizabeth, that woman makes me nervous. She's been spoilt' rotten and thinks she's better 'n anybody."

Elizabeth replied, "She reminds me of some of the girls I went to school with. Let's not be too critical of her. Miss Caldwell may not be happy with herself. We all have our cross to bear." How well Elizabeth knew that.

"Mary Lee, is she a relative of the Andrew Caldwell I met when we went on the picnic with Robert?"

"Captain Caldwell's her brother."

"I should have guessed from that thick auburn hair and green eyes."

"I don't know Captain Caldwell much. The ladies like him and I hear he's right nice. Too bad I cain't say the same fer his sister."

Elizabeth laughed. "As long as she spent the money she did, I can put up with her. If you don't have any plans, how would you like to be treated to dinner at the Virginia House?"

"I can pay fer my own," came Mary Lee's prideful reply. " I'm right hungry. We sure were busy all day."

"We were that. If I let you pay for your own dinner, then it wouldn't be my treat, would it? You were the one that trimmed up Ruth Caldwell's hat and I charged her extra. Look at it as a reward."

"I swear, Miz' Elizabeth, you do make me smile."

****

Saturday, Lloyd Pierce brought the mail by but Elizabeth was too busy to open it before she closed for the day.

She placed the closed sign in the window promptly at five o'clock before opening the day's mail. There were two catalogues and a letter with a return address of Georgetown hospital. She shook as she opened it.

October 15, 1916

Dear Miss Fairchilds,
This is to acknowledge we received your letter of inquiry, but there are no records regarding a Matthew Quinton Fairchilds.
Sincerely,
Jonathan Clark
Medical Records

Elizabeth read the terse note once again before she threw it across the counter. How could that be? There had to be records. A patient doesn't just vanish from a hospital. Tears came to her eyes

before she could stop them. She would get to the bottom of it.

34

After sitting and mulling over her problem, she let her mind drift. It was Saturday night, and here she was sitting alone in a dim hat shop with a blackened fireplace and the cold October night seeping in. With a mournful sigh, Elizabeth picked up the letter she had tossed and put it in her apron pocket. She would keep it for her records and begin her quest anew. Perhaps if she went to the hospital in person, it would make a difference. The uncertainty of not knowing what mattered most in her life gave her distress. Would she ever find her child?

Chapter 5

By the end of October, Elizabeth had pulled enough money together to take the train and spend two nights in Washington. The jewelry salesman was right. She had sold all she had ordered and had more coming for the Christmas season. The Harvest Party had brought in enough customers that the profit from the jewelry allowed two nights away without financially putting the shop in jeopardy. That evening she would ask Mary Lee to tend the shop until she returned so she could take the train the next day.

****

On Sunday afternoon, Herbert Marks pulled the long twelve-passenger automobile to the side of the street in front of the Berryville Hotel. Elizabeth was waiting. She carried a small satchel and handbag. Herbert asked if he could store the satchel for her but she declined. "No thank you, Mr. Marks. I prefer to hold it on my lap." The satchel contained everything she would need for her trip to the city and she was not going to take a chance on losing it.

There were passengers who had ridden down from the Winchester area causing her to take the last bench seat, which was fine with Elizabeth as long as she got to the train. This was her first trip to Washington by herself but she had made careful plans. Washington was not a foreign city to her. She felt confident that once she arrived, she could get to where she needed to go. Her stomach felt like it was tied up in knots. This was not a trip of pleasure and her search might prove to be in vain. Try as she did to rid her mind of that possibility, it nagged at her conscience.

Herbert announced they were ready to go. Elizabeth placed her satchel on the empty seat next to her.

Although she had a good view, there was no need to look at the scenery because the colors of fall had disappeared and there was a light mist in the air. She took her book from the satchel and began to read. When the car crossed the Shenandoah River Bridge and drove through the hamlet of Pine Grove, Elizabeth glanced out the window. On the other side of a stone fence, sheep were grazing in a brown field, their wool as dingy as the landscape. The long, black car went around a horseshoe curve and started its climb up the mountain.

Bluemont was a quiet little town on the east side of the Blue Ridge Mountains, where the Washington-Old Dominion Railway made a turn around to head the sixty miles back to the city.

There were fewer passengers and less activity than when Elizabeth and her parents had arrived in June. That was the time Washingtonians traveled west either to stay in the cooler temperatures of the mountains in Virginia or to go to the mineral baths in West Virginia.

The train was waiting. She bought her round trip ticket and went to the boarding platform. The conductor held her satchel and helped her step up into the rail coach. "Go right ahead, miss. We'll be leaving in a few minutes."

Taking a seat at the back of the car, Elizabeth hoped she would have the seat to herself. The schedule said they were to leave at three o'clock. Here they were ten minutes behind time. From the front of the car, the conductor announced that they had been waiting for one more passenger, and he had just arrived. They would leave as soon as he was on board.

Whoever it is must be someone important, thought Elizabeth. Scanning the seats in front of her, she noted they were all full except for one that held a large lady whose wide breadth covered the whole seat. Elizabeth's desire to ride without someone seated next to her was dashed. She felt a tug of chagrin before squeezing her satchel between the side of the rail car and her feet. She would just keep her nose in the book she had opened and disregard whoever the new passenger would be.

The conductor's voice carried through the car, "It's good to have you with us again, sir."

A man's pleasant voice replied," Hope I didn't hold you up. Ran into some problem along the way."

"Knew you would be along, sir. We're a few minutes behind but we'll do our best to make it up." Then, with a sly smile, he added, "We're rarely on time anyway."

The passenger came to the back of the car, where he stashed his travel bag behind the seat. "Afternoon, ma'am." Elizabeth glanced up from her book. "Why, Miss Fairchilds!" he exclaimed.

She was as surprised as he. "Captain Caldwell?" He looked so handsome and gallant in his uniform it caused her to catch her breath.

The train lurched forward as he swung into his seat. "It is most unexpected to find you here." He smiled and his green eyes twinkled. "We didn't have time for pleasant conversation when we met. Did you enjoy your picnic?"

Elizabeth cast her eyes downward. His congenial manner caused her to blush as she recalled how abrupt she had been that day.

"I did," she replied.

The seats were so close together that his shoulder brushed against hers. She was not going to sit pressed to his shoulder so she leaned into the side of the rail car as tightly as she could.

His long legs spilled under the seat in front of him. She sat upright as a board and he looked so relaxed he fairly melted into the seat. Was she going to be this uncomfortable all the way?

"What brings you to Washington, Miss Fairchilds? I assume that's where you're headed."

"Yes," she answered. "I have business to attend to."

"I understand you own the millinery shop in town."

"I do."

He laughed. "Don't you want to know how I gained that information?"

"No, sir. I assume that everyone in Clarke County knows everyone else's business." Her attention went back to her open book.

He laughed even more. "Miss Fairchilds, you wound me. Do you really want to have your nose in that book?"

"I find the book interesting," she replied without looking at him.

He placed his hand over his heart. "Oh, you've done it again."

Elizabeth closed the book and smiled at him. "Wounding a captain in the United States Cavalry? I may be trucked off to jail at the next stop."

From that moment, they seemed to have bridged a gap. By the time they reached Washington, they were on a first name basis.

"Where will you be staying while you're here?" he asked.

"I'll be at the Willard Hotel. It's a convenient spot for me to get the trolley to where I have to go."

Andrew asked," Why don't we have dinner together? I don't have to be back at the base until eight. That will give us a couple of hours."

Dining would be harmless because she didn't plan on seeing him again, and, she was famished. Plus, Andrew would insist on paying, which was an unexpected bonus, so she agreed.

When they reached the Alexandria station, Andrew hailed a cab and they were off to the hotel.

When they reached the Willard, he was treated like royalty. They walked up the front stone steps where the erect doorman greeted them. "Captain Caldwell, always good to see you, sir," he said as he opened the door.

Elizabeth felt her face color. Obviously Andrew had been here many times and probably with many different ladies. Well, it didn't matter. It would be the first and last time for her.

Andrew was allowed to carry her satchel only because he was adamant that ladies did not carry their own bags if there was a gentleman around to do it.

Elizabeth said, "I have acquiesced to your desire to carry my bag, but I am going to inquire if my room is waiting. They will store my bag while we eat."

"I'll be happy to check you in," Andrew replied.

"That isn't necessary."

Andrew could not be deterred. He held tight to her tapestry satchel as they neared the front desk in the opulently furnished lobby.

"Captain Caldwell. Welcome. What can I do for you, sir?"

"Hello, George. This lady is inquiring about a room reservation."

Without hesitation Elizabeth spoke up. "My name is Elizabeth Fairchilds and I have requested a room for tonight and tomorrow. Would you be so kind as to see if there is one under my name?"

The clerk became all business as he scanned his ledger. "Yes, Miss Fairchilds, Room 216 has been reserved for you. Do you have luggage that needs to go up?"

"I have only this satchel that Captain Caldwell has insisted on carrying."

With a grin, Andrew produced the bag.

Elizabeth continued, "Would you please store it for me until I am ready to go to my room?"

"Be happy to," said the clerk. He motioned to a colored bellhop to take the bag.

Elizabeth turned on her heel and walked away causing Andrew to catch up. In three long strides he was beside her with a big smile on his face. "Are you ready to enter the dining room, Miss Fairchilds?"

"If it was your intention to embarrass me, you succeeded." She kept her voice low, but the irritation was evident. "Perhaps dining together isn't such a good idea."

"I am sorry if I offended you. I was just enjoying the moment."

She stopped and looked directly at him. "I'd prefer that it wasn't at my expense."

"Do you always show this much spirit?" he asked.

She started toward the dining room. "Only when I have to."

"Well, I admire it," he said, as he looped his arm through hers. "You are familiar with this hotel."

"I used to come with my parents for special occasions. It doesn't escape me that you are recognized here, which tells me you are a frequent visitor."

They arrived at the entrance of the dining room where a stately waiter, clad in white jacket and black trousers, hurried to greet them.

"Good evening, Captain Caldwell. Would you like your favorite table?"

"That would be nice," answered Andrew.

As the waiter was escorting them to their table, Elizabeth gave Andrew a wry smile and whispered, "You seem to be a prize patron."

The table was covered with a spotless white tablecloth and a candle glowed from a glass holder. The tall window next to it was decorated with gold brocade drapes.

"This is a lovely spot," remarked Elizabeth.

"That's why it's my favorite. It's more private than being out on the main floor."

The waiter placed menus before them.

"What's good this evening, Harry?" asked Andrew.

"I would recommend the crab served with a creamy sauce over rice with peas and carrots for the vegetable."

"Elizabeth would you care for a glass of wine," asked Andrew. "The house wine is excellent."

She would love a glass of wine, but after the long ride, and an empty stomach, she was afraid

43

it would make her giddy. "No, thank you. I would like a cup of hot tea."

"There you have it, Harry. Tea for the lady and a heady glass of wine for me."

The waiter left to get the drinks while they looked over the menu.

"Will you be having the crab? " Elizabeth asked. "I believe I will settle for the beef roast with vegetables."

"A good choice," he responded. "I had plenty of beef, pork and chicken at the Harvest Party while I was at home, so I'm off for something more adventurous. Harry has never steered me wrong."

"I'd like to hear more about this Harvest Party. It must be the highlight of the year for some."

"That it is. Perhaps someday you will attend."

The waiter returned with their drinks and took their order before he disappeared.

Andrew took a sip of wine and studied her over his glass. "My mother's middle name is Elizabeth, Virginia Elizabeth Caldwell."

"Do you favor her or your father?"

"Definitely my mother. She has the auburn hair and green eyes. I guess my height comes from her side also because I'm a good deal taller than my father."

"Do you have brothers and sisters?"

"One brother and one sister."

"Ruth?"

This piqued his interest. He leaned forward. "You've met my sister?"

"She came into the shop one day."

He eyed her carefully. "What did you think of her?"

Elizabeth felt her face beginning to warm and chose her words with care. "She is attractive and she was a good customer."

He covered her hand with his. "You mean she was difficult to please, but spent a lot of money."

"That would be another way to put it."

"I know Ruth. She's been spoiled."

Elizabeth smiled at the very words Mary Lee had used. She was conscious of his hand on hers so she slipped it out to hold her teacup with both hands.

He took the hint and settled back in his chair. "And, what about you, Miss Fairchilds? What about your family? You're quite mysterious."

"Mysterious? I'm flattered."

"A fetching, refined and educated young lady ends up in a small town, where it seems no one knows her, and buys her own business. I call that mysterious."

The waiter interrupted with their meals, which gave Elizabeth some time to form an explanation.

Once the waiter left, Andrew continued, "As we were saying…"

"I'm an only child. I have always lived in the Washington area, and I went to a private school.

When I finished, my parents thought the hat shop was a good investment so they bought it for me."

He was skeptical. "Seventy miles away? They must have wanted to get rid of you," he laughed.

More than you know, thought she.

Andrew wasn't through with his questions. "No marriage prospects? Once out of finishing school girls are looking for a well-heeled man, or so I'm told."

"None," she replied. "I guess my father found out about the hat shop from an acquaintance."

"Still, it's quite unusual. Are you happy with it?"

She wanted to jump up and shout, "No, I don't like it or being away from the city or having to do everything for myself." Instead she replied, "It seems to be working out."

He gave a pensive look. "I'm quite pleased with my career, but lately, I've had the feeling that something is missing. I can't put my finger on it. It's just an unsettled feeling."

With a wry smile, she said, "I understand."

When they finished their meal, Andrew escorted her from the dining room, and before he left to return to the base, he kissed her hand. "Thank you for a most enjoyable day, Elizabeth. I trust you will have a good visit."

"Goodbye, Andrew. It was nice to have your company."

With an unexpected twinge of regret, she watched the august Captain Caldwell walk away.

Chapter 6

The next morning Elizabeth was up early after having spent a fitful night. No matter which way she turned or how many sheep she'd counted, sleep eluded her. She pressed a cold washcloth to her eyes and forehead. Her mind must be clear for what lay ahead.

The hotel room was chilly. She dressed quickly smoothing out any wrinkles as best she could from the same long navy crepe skirt she had worn the day before. Her lacy, long sleeved, white waist was fresh and smelled of lavender. She wanted to look feminine and business-like at the same time. Care was taken to tuck her blonde hair under the brown velvet saucer hat she wore. Throwing a tan camelhair coat over her arm, she pronounced herself ready. Out the door she went before turning to lock it and dropped the key into a section of her large pocketbook.

She was waiting for her breakfast to be served in the dining room of the hotel when a gentleman stopped by her table and asked if she would like some company. Her answer was a cold stare and he moved on. Although her stomach was doing little flips, she knew she had to eat a good breakfast to get through the day. She ordered eggs, bacon, toast and fried apples with a cup of coffee.

Tea was her beverage of choice but she wanted the extra energy that coffee seemed to bring.

One more check in her purse to be sure Johnathan Clark's letter was there before she left the dining room, and she was on her way to wait for the trolley that would take her to the Georgetown Hospital.

On the trolley, she watched as well-dressed gentlemen walked the streets on their way to work, many of them heading for the government buildings. She rehearsed over and over in her mind what she would say when she got to the hospital. When her stop was announced, she offered a silent prayer before stepping off the trolley and onto the street. It was a two-block walk to the hospital in the invigorating crisp morning air.

At the hospital, she walked through the double doors and went to the information desk. The day help had just come on duty. A middle-aged lady sat behind a desk. "Yes, miss. May I help you?"

"I need to find the records department."

"Do you have an appointment?"

"No, ma'am. I didn't realize that was necessary. I have come a long way, so it is imperative that I see someone today. I am willing to wait."

"They are always quite busy, but I'll direct you to that department and you can try."

Elizabeth gave her a relieved smile. "Thank you. I can't ask for more than that."

The helpful receptionist pointed to her left. "Straight down this hallway, take the first left and the records room is the second door on the right."

Elizabeth was off with renewed spring in her step. The second door on the right was clearly marked, Records Department. She didn't know if she should knock or just enter. When a polite rap on the door brought no response, she turned the knob and went in. It looked a bit disorganized with files laying on counters and desktops, but there were rows and rows on long shelves that looked orderly, much like a library.

There was a bell on the counter that read, *Ring bell for assistance*. Gingerly, she did as it said. In the stillness of the room, the bell sounded like the clanging of a fire engine to her anxious ears. A gray head sprang up from behind one of the counters.

"And, what is it you need so early in the morning? Haven't time to waste, you know."

His manner gave her pause. She cleared her throat and pulled the letter from her purse. "My name is Elizabeth Fairchilds and I am here to inquire about records for a baby boy, Matthew Quinton Fairchilds. Here is the letter sent to me by Johnathan Clark stating there are no records by that name."

"If I sent that to you, then there are no records. What makes you think otherwise?"

Irritation was creeping into her voice, and she did not want to alienate the man, "Because he was born in this hospital. There have to be records. Is there someone else I might speak to who can give me an explanation?"

His tone lost its acetic quality. "I'm sorry, Miss Fairchilds, but I am the manager in charge of the records. I can only say, again, there are no records here regarding that name."

She stood for a minute fighting back tears. "Thank you, Mr. Clark. I'm sorry to have bothered you."

Once outside she sat on a bench in the hallway dabbing at her eyes. A young man stopped before opening the door to the records room. "Is there anything I can do for you?"

"I have come all this way to find records on my child and there are none. I do not understand how that could be."

The young man sat down beside her. "Was your child ill?"

"No, he was born here."

"What is your son's name?"

"Matthew Quinton Fairchilds," she replied. "He was born last April."

He lowered his voice to a confidential tone. "Miss Fairchilds, I work in records. I can tell you we have no information, but I can also tell you that money and influence are great bargainers. My advice is to talk with your parents."

"My parents? What good would that do?"

"That is all I can say. I remember the case very well. I would appreciate it if you would keep this chat confidential."

"I am confused, but I guess I have no choice. My parents and I are not on the best of terms."

The young man stood up. " I believe they are your only hope. I wish you luck." He turned the handle of the door to the records department and disappeared.

Elizabeth sat in a daze. What could be the reason he would remember a child's name? There are babies born here all the time. Did Edward have that much influence? The mention of the father of her child brought only feelings of disgust and shame. A thought passed through her mind. Records could not be destroyed but they could be hidden.

If she must face her parents then she would have to get on with it; such a prospect seemed formidable.

At one-thirty in the afternoon, Elizabeth was climbing the six steps leading up to the large covered porch that spanned the stately white house in Alexandria where she'd grown up. The familiar porch swing was still there. The swing she and her friend, Madeline, had swung in, sung in, and played cats in the cradle. Madeline had never been healthy and died when she was eleven. That was the first devastating loss for Elizabeth, until her grandmother died the next year, and then her parents bundled her off to the private school.

She hesitated before ringing the doorbell. It was a thick oak door with a large leaded glass window. There was one clear corner in the right side that, if you twisted your head a certain way, you could peek in and see down the hallway. She rang the bell again.

On the second ring, a colored maid opened the door.

"Yes, miss? Then came the recognition but she kept her voice low. "Oh, Lordy, Lordy! It's you Miz' Elizabeth. You come right in here and let me look at you." She took both of Elizabeth's hands in hers turning her this way and that. "Beautiful, that's what you are." And then, this woman, who had been a significant part of her life, pulled her into her arms as though she would never let her go.

Elizabeth whispered, "You're squeezing me, Opal. I can't breathe."

The overjoyed woman released her grip. "I'm just so happy to see you. How have you been, child?"

Elizabeth sighed, "Life has changed much for me, but I am learning to tolerate it. Are my parents home?"

The joy in Opal dissolved. "Your momma is upstairs in her room." She took Elizabeth's hands in hers. "But, child, she said that if you ever come to the house, she won't see you."

"Now that isn't her choice, is it? I'm here and I'm going up!"

"Miz' Elizabeth, you can't go against her wishes."

"Just this once, Opal, I'm going to." Elizabeth rushed up the stairs before Opal could bar her way.

She gave a knock and then opened the door to her mother's room. Gertrude Fairchilds was sitting at a secretary's desk writing. She didn't look up. Apparently, she had heard the conversation with Opal.

"Hello, Mother."

"Hello, Elizabeth. How is the hat shop?"

"It was fine when I left."

"That's good."

Elizabeth stood just inside the door. "I don't understand why I haven't heard a word from you or father since you abandoned me in that lonely place. Aren't you even curious as to why I'm here?"

"Not especially."

"How long did you think it would be before I came searching for my son?"

At that, her mother put the pen down and turned to face her daughter. It was many silent seconds before she spoke.

"Are you out of your mind? That chapter in your life is over. Do you hear me? Your father and I did what was best for you."

Elizabeth gained courage and ventured a few steps into the room. "I've been to the hospital. They say there are no records."

Her mother stood up. "If that's what they say, then I'm sure that's true."

"I've found out otherwise. I was told you can help me."

Her mother's gaze was intense. "Help you what? Ruin any prospects you may still have for a decent life? Forget the past, Elizabeth! I have nothing more to say."

"Forget?" Elizabeth heard her voice rising. "How can I forget? You forced that man on me. I regret that I was so inexperienced, but you should have realized. Forget that I almost died giving birth to a child I have never seen? How do you forget you have a child? I guess in your case it works."

Gertrude Fairchilds turned her back on her daughter and went back to sit at her desk.

Elizabeth was furious. She fled out of the room slamming the door behind her. Down the stairs she sped. Her hand was on the door handle when another hand covered hers. She heard the words, "Child, come with me," whispered into her ear.

Elizabeth recognized Opal's voice and released her grip on the door handle. Opal put her finger to her lips. The maid opened and shut the front door giving the impression Elizabeth had left before ushering her down the hallway to the kitchen. Closing the door behind them, the kind maid said in a low, controlled voice, "Come and sit at the table while I fix us both a cup of tea."

"I have to get back to the hotel."

Opal guided her to a chair. "You have time for tea to settle you down. Then you need to listen to what I have to say."

Elizabeth took a seat with some reluctance. Opal put her hands on her shoulders. "You're so upset, you're shaking. You must calm yourself."

Elizabeth was on the verge of tears. "Opal, I feel so lost."

"Of course you do. Your momma thought she was doing the right thing by you. She has always been so upright she didn't know what else to do."

"It was her fault, Opal. She pushed that man on me. All she wanted was to get me married off to a man of substance, as she called it. She didn't much care what he was like."

Opal poured the tea and took a seat opposite Elizabeth. "Child, you know that servants hear a lot of what's going on but keep their mouths shut."

"I know that," she replied.

"You need to hear this. When you were in the hospital, Mr. Edward came by the house. I heard him talking to your parents. He said he was sorry, but he had never intended marriage or getting saddled with a baby. He handed them an envelope and said there was enough money in it to take care of you and to place the baby somewhere."

Elizabeth was numb. "Do you mean that my parents took the money, said thank you, and he just left?"

"Not before your momma lit into him and your daddy had to hold her back. She told him there was no amount of money in the world that could undo the grief he'd caused. Then your daddy ordered Mr. Edward out of the house and told him never to come back."

Elizabeth slumped in her chair. "So they found the hat shop for sale and paid for it with the money Edward had given them."

"I 'spect, but I don't know that. What I do know is, I heard them talking about a lawyer who said he could place the baby in an orphanage until he could be adopted."

"Oh, my God!" cried Elizabeth. "He could be anywhere!"

"Shush, child. If your momma knows we've been talking, she'll get rid of me for sure."

Elizabeth settled into a calmer state. "Do you know the lawyer's name or if the orphanage is in Washington?"

"I 'spect that its hereabouts. But, Miz' Elizabeth, your baby would be six months old. Most likely he's not there anymore."

Elizabeth rose from her chair, "Thank you for telling me, Opal. I must be leaving. I am not going to give up until I know where he is."

Opal came around the table and gave her a hug. "You take care of yourself, Miz' Elizabeth. I hope you find your baby. I surely do."

The back door closed quietly as Elizabeth left the only home she'd ever known. She wondered if her mother was watching her walk down the sidewalk, but she refused to look up.

****

By the time the trolley arrived near the Willard the dusk of evening had fallen. Elizabeth hurried along the dimly lit street and hurried into the warmth and safety of the huge hotel.

In the lobby, George, the desk clerk, stopped her. "Miss Fairchilds, before going to your room, there's a small package for you. If you can wait, I'll get it."

The attractive package was wrapped in foil paper and tied with a mauve ribbon. She hustled up to her room wondering who could have sent it.

She unlocked the door and once inside the room, she threw her coat on the bed, eager to open the package and see what it held. She undid the ribbon and tore off the wrapping. It contained a small box. Lifting the lid, she found a miniature crystal vase filled with delicate dried flowers. There was a note:

> *Dear Elizabeth,*
>
> *Please accept this small memento as a thank you for the pleasant time we shared.*
>
> *I wish you a safe trip back home.*
> *My fondest regards,*
> *Andrew*

The gift brought a smile to her face as she carefully placed it in her satchel. Andrew could never guess how welcome this small act of thoughtfulness gave such a warm feeling to drown out her cares of the day. Elizabeth had spent a day of defeat, but there was a small window of hope. Would it be enough?

Chapter 7

Andrew Caldwell stretched out his six-foot frame on his cot in the officers' quarters. Hands under his head and crossed legs, he was lying there sorting out the thoughts that wouldn't go away.

First was the war in Europe. The U.S. Government had sent many dollars worth of aid to their allies, and, although the country had managed to stay out of the conflict, would the next step be sending the military?

Then there was that nagging irritation he couldn't describe. It was an uncomfortable feeling that had bothered him for the past few months.

Finally, what about Elizabeth Fairchilds? She was the most puzzlement of all. Andrew had known many young ladies and moved on without a second thought. But, to his annoyance, Elizabeth lingered in his mind.

He rose from the cot. The uniform he would wear to the commandant's meeting in the morning was impeccably pressed. His boots could use a shine.

Taking a white rag and a can of saddle soap, he started the job. Expending energy on a mindless task might ease his unsettled feeling. He buffed and polished until the boots shone.

By eleven o'clock, he lay back on the cot hoping for sleep. It was slow in coming.

To his surprise, in the morning, he awoke refreshed. At six-thirty, he was fully dressed and went down to the kitchen for breakfast. The smell of perked coffee quickened his step. He filled a mug before taking his seat at the table with three other officers.

A lieutenant across from Andrew looked up. "Going to the general's party?" he asked. A sly smile slid across his face.

"Not much of a party," Andrew answered.

"Suppose he's going to brief you on how the war is going?"

Andrew answered cautiously, "I'm not sure what he has in mind for this meeting."

The cook set their plates before them. "Eat heartily, sirs. The way we're sending supplies overseas there won't be nothin' left here at home."

The chatty lieutenant picked up on the conversation. "Looks to me," he said, "like Wilson isn't going to be able to keep us out of this war. We'll all be going over and sooner than we think."

Andrew shot him a dark glance. "Those are dangerous words. It isn't up to us to speculate and get rumors started. Until President Wilson makes a formal declaration of war, we are standing by and aiding our allies."

The piercing look from his green eyes was enough to silence the lieutenant. The other men nodded in agreement and finished their breakfasts without further comment.

Andrew took his hat from the peg beside the door and placed it on his head before he went out into the cool morning air. It was early, but he knew Asa and Carolyn would be up as Asa had been summoned to the general's meeting also. Andrew was sure Carolyn would not let her husband leave without a good breakfast.

He strode the two blocks to the small, two-story, brick house, which Asa was fortunate to have provided by the army. He had earned it after completing a dangerous mission.

Andrew sometimes resented having to live in a house with three others, but it was a step up from the barracks.

He knocked on the door, which was opened by Carolyn. She held the baby in her arms. "Andrew, you're early. Asa is upstairs getting dressed, but I'm delighted to see you. Come in and have a cup of coffee while I fry up some eggs and bacon."

He stepped inside. "I'll take the coffee but I just finished breakfast. May I hold Ann Catherine while you prepare for Asa?"

"That would be a help. Here, sit in this chair, and I'll drape a cloth over your uniform. You wouldn't want her to spit up on you."

He chuckled. "No, I don't think the general would understand."

Carolyn placed the baby in the crook of his arm as he sat at the table. He looked down at the little one swaddled in a warm blanket.

"She's grown, Carolyn."

The proud mother smiled as she busied herself about the stove.

"Yes, she likes her milk. You haven't been around for a couple of weeks, Andrew. What have you been doing with yourself?"

He tenderly traced the baby's cheek with his finger. "I went back home for a few days for the harvest celebration. Remember?"

Carolyn stopped and gazed out the window as if to recall a scene. "The first time I met Asa was at one of your harvest parties." She smiled at the memory. "How is your mother?"

"Doing quite well. It was you who nursed her back to health. Father asked about you."

Carolyn cracked the eggs and beat them with a wire whisk. "That was kind of him. He was always considerate. How is Ruth? She and I never seemed to be comfortable with each other."

Andrew pulled the baby in front of him to his lap and held her while he studied her face. "Well, you know Ruth. I pity the man who marries her."

"Maybe she'll change."

"Not likely," he said. "I don't know if this little one favors you or Asa."

Carolyn came over to peer down at her four-month old child. "We both have the dark hair and dark eyes, so she didn't have much of a choice there. Look, she's smiling at you."

"All the girls smile at me," he quipped. "Better she looks like her mother than her father."

"What's that I hear?" came a booming voice from the stairs.

61

Asa came into the kitchen and Andrew kept his eyes on the baby. "We were discussing your lovely little daughter. I remarked that it was better for her to look like her mother."

"I agree," answered Asa, and kissed his wife on the cheek. "Breakfast smells great." He poured himself a large mug of coffee before he sat his strapping frame at the table. He had dark, penetrating eyes and this morning they looked concerned. "What do you expect we're going to hear from the old man this morning? It's certainly been kept hush-hush. I'm not ready to hear that we're about to be shipped off to Europe, Andrew."

Carolyn put her husband's breakfast in front of him and took the baby from Andrew's arms. "I don't care to hear that kind of talk."

"Yes, let's talk about something pleasant," said Andrew, and changed the subject. "Carolyn, do you know Elizabeth Fairchilds?"

"The young lady that bought Catherine's hat shop?"

"That would be the young lady."

"I just caught a quick look when she came with her parents; curly hair, attractive, rather a doleful little thing who looked out of place."

"I met her at the Mitchells'. She was with Mary Lee Thompson, who's courting a new man at the Mitchell place. All three had come out for a picnic. She was sitting under a big oak tree reading a book and didn't give me the time of day. As luck would have it, I rode into Washington on the train with her, and we had dinner at the Willard."

Carolyn sat as if waiting to hear more. "And, that's it?"

"That's it."

Asa had been quiet to this point. "Why are you telling us this, Andrew?"

"Because it bothers me that I can't figure out why a refined, educated, attractive, young lady from the city would be running a hat shop in Berryville."

Asa was busy devouring his breakfast. "Did you ask her?" the pragmatic captain questioned.

"Well, of course I asked her," Andrew said, "and she didn't give me a direct answer." He leaned back in his chair as though defeated.

Carolyn held the baby and, in a teasing voice, said, "Oh, Captain Caldwell. I think you are smitten."

Before he could respond, Asa clasped him on the shoulder. "Come on friend. I've finished my breakfast. It's time for us to find out what the general has up his sleeve."

No sooner had the two men left than Carolyn went to the telephone. She was overjoyed to hear the voice on the other end answer, "Burke residence."

"Catherine, this is Carolyn. I hope I didn't call too early."

"I'm having breakfast."

"I can call back."

"No, if this is important enough to call me this early, then I need to hear it."

"I just had to tell you. Do you know Andrew Caldwell?"

"You know I do."

In a conspiratorial voice, Carolyn said, "You're not going to believe this, but, Andrew has met the young lady who bought your hat shop and he is enamored with her."

Catherine laughed. "If I recall, Andrew Caldwell is enamored with most young ladies he meets."

"No, this is different, I can tell. Do you know why she bought your shop?"

"I think her parents were the ones with the capital. If there is any unsavory reason behind it, it is none of our business. She seemed like a sweet person."

Carolyn persisted, "Yes, but don't you think it odd that she left the city to go out there, where she's a stranger? I think there's more to the story."

"I swear, Carolyn. You're beginning to sound like Lavinia Talley."

She bristled at the comparison, "This isn't like Lavinia's prattle. Andrew and Asa are like brothers. If Andrew is interested in Elizabeth, and I'm sure he is, then I want her to be the right person for him."

"Carolyn, my friend, it's none of our business. If something comes from Andrew's infatuation, then it will work out." To switch the tone of the conversation, she asked, "How is Ann Catherine?"

"I'm holding her this minute. She's growing everyday. We must get together or your godchild will be walking before you know it. You spend entirely too much time in that hat shop."

Catherine sighed. "I know. The shop is doing well and with Patrick back in medical school, it keeps me occupied."

"You'll end up a doctor's widow. He'll be gone more than he's home."

"Just as you've experienced as a soldier's wife?"

"Well, that's true. Now, what are we going to do about Elizabeth Fairchilds?" Carolyn asked.

"We are not going to do anything," Catherine answered with finality. "If you and Asa don't have any plans, how would you like to come and spend Thanksgiving Day with us?"

"Aren't you spending it with Patrick's family?"

"Since his mother passed away, we don't get to see Liam and Sarah that often. They are going to Sarah's parents' house. We were invited but her parents are a bit too stuffy for me. I would much prefer to spend it with good friends."

"Catherine, we would love to come. Thank you for asking. Is there anything I can bring?"

"Do you still bake those delicious custard pies?"

"I most certainly do."

"Good. Bring one along." In a teasing voice she added, "You can bring Andrew Caldwell along and we'll spend the afternoon pumping him with questions about his intentions concerning Elizabeth Fairchilds."

Carolyn laughed. "Catherine, you do bring me back to earth. What time shall we come on Thanksgiving?"

"Two o'clock."

"That's perfect. We will see you then. Goodbye, Catherine."

"Goodbye, Carolyn."

Chapter 8

When Elizabeth returned to Berryville on Tuesday, she was hungry and spent. It had been a tiring two days, but it hadn't been in vain because she was heartened to know that her child had lived. When he was born, she was so ill she didn't remember anything that had happened. And, when she was recuperating at home, there was not a word mentioned about the baby so she thought the infant had died. She had felt so ashamed and guilt-ridden she dared not ask. A pall hung over the house during those sad and depressing days.

Now Elizabeth knew the truth and she was determined to scout every orphanage she could find.

As she crossed the street from Herbert Marks' long car, the odor of food from the Virginia House made her realize how hungry she was. She opened the door to her apartment, hung her coat on a peg on the coat rack, turned on the dim light over the stairs and hurried on up to find something to eat. There was peanut butter and jelly in the cupboard and some crackers in the drawer. To her surprise there was a note on the table that read:

I made the stew and pie today. Robert helpt. Glad for you to be home. Your friend, Mary Lee.

The note brought a smile to Elizabeth's face. She suspected it wouldn't be too much longer before

Robert asked Mary Lee to marry him. And any man that was as attentive and helpful as he would make a good husband. Elizabeth was hopeful for Mary Lee's sake.

After devouring the stew and a couple of crackers, she took the piece of apple pie from the icebox, brewed a cup of tea and went into the living room to eat. Robert had left a low fire in the fireplace. With a fire burning, it was good she hadn't been delayed. Sitting down on the chintz flowered couch, she spied her satchel on the floor in the hall and remembered Andrew's gift. Putting her dessert aside, Elizabeth brought the bag into the living room where she proceeded to take out the small crystal vase filled with delicate dried flowers. She placed it on the windowsill. It brightened the room causing a smile to spread as she recalled the pleasant time she had spent with Andrew Caldwell.

****

The next morning Elizabeth was busy dusting the shop when the jewelry salesman came by.

"Good morning, Miss Fairchilds. This will be the last order before Christmas so you'll want to have plenty of inventory on hand. You'll find that you'll need to make your money before the holidays end because winter months are lean."

Elizabeth knew he was right. The first order of jewelry had sold well and increased her boldness in deciding what she would order this time around.

Income from the first jewelry sales had allowed her the trip to Washington without having to withdraw any money from her bank account. Giving the purchase some thought, she reasoned, if she put most of her money into jewelry and accessories, she would realize more income than from the sale of hats. It was a gamble. Regardless, she gave the ever-encouraging salesman an order for all but twenty-five dollars in her bank account.

He grinned from ear to ear. "No ma'am. You're not going to be a bit sorry. It's the sign of a shrewd business woman."

Once he packed up his samples and was out the door, Eizabeth sank into a nearby chair. She had been swept away with the glib salesman's patter and his alluring displays of jewelry. The thought struck her that she may have impulsively bought herself into ruin. It was too unsettling to dwell on it.

Elizabeth busied herself around the shop and felt a sense of relief when Mary Lee Thompson walked in the door. As it usually happened, when she appeared the whole day seemed to brighten.

Chapter 9

The next week brought two welcome packages. One was a large box with hats sent by Catherine Burke.

> *November 1, 1916*
>
> *Dear Miss Fairchilds,*
>
> *I am sending this inventory of hats that have become out of style in Washington. I am sure they will sell in Berryville. Some finishing touches are required, but they will be most handsome when completed.*
>
> *I realize this is presumptuous of me to send them on without asking. They are a tasteful selection and are of no use sitting in my storeroom.*
>
> *I trust all is well. Perhaps we could get together if you are ever in the city.*
>
> *Sincerely,*
>
> *Catherine Burke*

Elizabeth opened the box without delay as soon as the postman left the shop. Inside she counted thirteen hats. They were an array of colors, but all winter materials. Some of her apprehension about ordering so much jewelry waned as she realized the hats would be added income.

The second package looked like a suitcase and was more difficult to open. With the help of scissors and a knife, she was pleased to see it filled with the jewelry she had ordered the week before. The salesman hadn't lost any time.

Elizabeth was in the process of unpacking when Mary Lee came by.

"I'm glad you're here. Look at this!" said Elizabeth, waving her hand over some eye-catching gems.

"Land sakes!" responded Mary Lee when she saw the package of jewelry. "I don't mean to talk out of turn, Miz' Elizabeth, but can you afford all this?"

Mary Lee's practical exclamation, only served to heighten Elizabeth's own self-doubt. She chewed on a fingernail while surveying her purchase before she replied, "This batch is paid for, but if you're asking if I can sell it all before I go under, the answer is, I don't know."

"Well the jewelry is right pretty" Mary Lee acknowledged as she started picking through the boxed pieces. She held up fake emerald earrings to her ear. "What do you think of these? Maybe I could hint to Robert to buy them for me for Christmas."

"Good idea," said Elizabeth as she dug down between some boxes and pulled out a matching necklace. "While he's at it, he can buy this." She held it for Mary Lee to marvel over.

Snatching the necklace from her friend's hand, Mary Lee was clasping it around her neck as she rushed to the mirror to admire it. "Why if that ain't the grandest thing I've ever seen." Her blue eyes were round as saucers. "I'll just bet if we can get the people into the shop, you can sell all of it."

Elizabeth sat in a chair behind the work counter while Mary Lee continued with her self-admiration in front of the mirror. "How do you propose that I get the word out that I have the jewelry for sale?"

Mary Lee came and took a seat opposite her. "I don't rightly know. I'd have to think on that."

"Well, I have been thinking about it, and this is what I'm going to do. I'm going to ask Mr. Talley to come over and help me compose a notice to put in the *Clarke Courier*. While he's here, we can get him to buy something for Lavinia. She'd be showing it off all over town before the paper comes out."

"That's for sure," agreed Mary Lee. "But, Mr. Talley's pretty tight with his money. I doubt he'll buy anythin'."

"We'll use our feminine wiles," Elizabeth laughed.

"Maybe, if I knew what that meant," said Mary Lee.

Elizabeth clapped her hands together as she rose from the chair. "It's a wonderful idea. Come and help me pick out a big gaudy pin. We can tell him this jewelry is all the rage in Paris."

"Paris?" Mary Lee gave a dubious look. "You mean that place over on the mountain?"

"No, Mary Lee, Paris, France. Lavinia will think she's one step up on every lady in the county."

The dubious Mary Lee ventured over to the pile of jewelry. "But, is that right? I mean, Miz' Elizabeth, it's like tellin' a fib."

Elizabeth stopped fumbling through the boxes to look at her friend. "Mary Lee, do you know if they are wearing this kind of jewelry in Paris?"

"No."

"Well neither do I, but they could be so I'll say that I bet it's all the rage in Paris and that way it won't be a fib. Does that make you feel better?"

Her friend looked skeptical.

"Oh, come on. It will be fine. It's time for a cup of tea. I want to read your tealeaves. I want to see if I can still find that ring."

"See if you can find one of them Paris women wearin' a big pin. That would make me feel better," said Mary Lee as the two young women made their way to the back room of the hat shop.

Elizabeth stood on her tiptoes to reach the can of tea biscuits, while Mary Lee put the kettle over.

"Do you want peanut butter or jam for your biscuits?" she asked.

"What kind of jam?"

"Strawberry."

73

"I'll take some strawberry," replied Mary Lee. "I don't like blackberry because them little seeds get into my teeth."

Elizabeth took a knife from a drawer. "I don't eat blackberry anymore because I dropped some on a white waist I was wearing and I never got the stain out. That was the end of blackberry jam for me."

Mary Lee put tealeaves into their cups before she poured the boiling water over them. After letting them steep, she skimmed off the leaves that floated to the top then took a seat at the table where Elizabeth was busy slathering jam on their biscuits.

"Do you want me to start decoratin' them hats Miz' Catherine sent you?"

Offering a biscuit, Elizabeth replied, "That would be wonderful. It'll give me time to decide how to display the jewelry. I have to write a thank you note to Mrs. Burke for so generous a contribution. I can't believe she doesn't want something in return."

"If you knew Miz' Catherine better, you'd know she don't 'spect' nothin' in return."

Elizabeth gave it some thought. "I would like to give her a piece of jewelry. Do you think she would like that?"

"I think she would like that right fine. Are you goin' back to the city agin'?"

The question caught her off guard. "Why do you ask?"

"Well, 'cause, if you are goin' back, I think Miz' Catherine would be pleased to have you go see her new shop. I wish I could go."

"But, why can't you go?"

"I don't know anythin' 'bout the city and Robert don't neither."

Elizabeth felt a tug at her heart. "Would you like to go with me, if I go?"

Mary Lee was cautious. "I don't know 'bout that."

"I'll tell you what. If we can sell all of this jewelry and these hats, we can make enough money so we could go for two or three days after Christmas. No one around here will care if the shop is closed at that time." She threw in an enticement. "The city will still be decorated for the holidays. We could have a wonderful time. What do you say?"

"I'm not sure."

"It will be my present to you."

"That's a mighty big present."

Elizabeth was enthused. "I can't make the money to do it without your help, and, if we make the money I hope we do, I can easily pay the way."

"I can pay some of it," came Mary Lee's prideful reply.

"Then let's start planning. We've got five weeks before Christmas."

Elizabeth held out her hand. "Is it a deal?"

Her enthusiasm was contagious. "It's a deal," Mary Lee replied as she took her friend's outstretched hand.

She had finished her tea down to a few drops and swished the cup three times. Without disturbing the leaves, she handed the cup to Elizabeth. "I hope there's nothin'bad in there."

After a full two minutes, without any word, Mary Lee was getting antsy. "Do you see that ring?"

"No," replied Elizabeth, "but I see a suitcase and smoke coming out of a train engine."

"Yer just sayin' that 'cause we talked about goin' to the city."

"Now, Mary Lee, you had better not start disbelieving the leaves," she said in a teasing voice. "Miss Elizabeth Fairchilds knows all."

Mary Lee rolled her eyes.

Chapter 10

The Monday before Thanksgiving, the tall, angular Lloyd Pierce brought the mail by. Elizabeth hadn't given Thanksgiving much thought because she had plans of working in the shop. There was much to do.

"Catalog and a letter for you today, Miss Fairchilds," he said as he handed her the mail. Then his eye caught the jewelry she had carefully placed near the window so the light would catch the gems. "Oh my gosh. Is that what was in that big box I brought over last week?"

"Yes, it was. You might keep this jewelry in mind if you are looking for a present for Mrs. Pierce."

"She does like that kind of stuff."

Elizabeth continued now that she had his attention. "Many of these are one of a kind. Once its gone there won't be another to replace it."

He gave her a sideways grin. "So what yer sayin' is that I'd better get it early."

"I'd be happy to put any piece back and save it for you, if you'd like."

"I've got to keep on my rounds, but I'd like to come back and take some time to look it over," he replied.

Elizabeth called after him when he opened the door to leave, "You won't be sorry, Mr. Pierce."

She took her seat behind the counter and prepared to open the letter Lloyd Pierce had left. When she saw the return address on the back, it gave her a start. She hurried to open it with her silver letter opener.

November 19, 1916

Dear Elizabeth,

Your father and I have decided to come to Berryville to spend Thanksgiving Day with you.

We are also interested in how the shop is doing and pray that you have become settled in the quaint little town. Also, we hope that you are making many acquaintances, which will be very useful for your business.

We have made arrangements to stay over at the Berryville Hotel. Would you be so kind as to be sure the room is secured for us?

We will arrive on Wednesday afternoon around four in the afternoon. Our train for the return trip is scheduled to leave on Friday at two o'clock.

Although it will be a short visit, we will be able to spend the holiday together.

Our best regards,
Mother

Thanksgiving Day? That was only three days away. As she sat with letter in hand, her emotions ran the gamut from disbelief to irritation to panic. It was as if the volatile encounter she'd had with her mother didn't exist. Thanksgiving dinner? Her mind was a whirl of thoughts. What did she know about cooking a turkey!

Elizabeth reread the letter. What would be the reasoning for her mother's change of heart, especially since they had had such an unpleasant meeting when she went to Alexandria? Elizabeth didn't believe that it was out of concern for her. There must be some other motivation driving her mother. After all, wasn't it her parents who dumped her into this town six months ago without her consent? And, wasn't it just like her mother to tell her they were coming without even asking? Well, they would find a different Elizabeth... or was it more likely she would crumble and acquiesce as she always had? It was too much to think about.

Elizabeth checked the clock. It was close to noon. She put the closed for lunch sign in the window and prepared to walk over to the Berryville Hotel to ask if her parents' room had been reserved. It was a sunny day and warm enough that she needed only a shawl. The hotel staff was busy cleaning and scurrying about when she entered.

"Good afternoon, Miss Fairchilds. What can I do for you?" asked the desk clerk.

"Good afternoon. I came to inquire if my parents' request for a reservation has arrived, and if there is a room available for them."

"Yes ma'am. I can answer that question right away. They have a room assigned. It's good that your mother called. We are quite busy with guests visiting for the Thanksgiving holiday."

"She telephoned?"

"Yes ma'am. A few days ago."

Elizabeth tried to repress the resentment building within. Her mother could call the hotel but couldn't make the effort to call her daughter?

She could smell food cooking triggering an idea to pop into her mind. "Do they serve dinner here at The Virginia House on Thanksgiving Day?"

"They do. And I have to say it is far better than what my wife puts on the table." He laughed at his own attempt at humor.

"I expect you will have quite a few out of town guests staying here." She gave him a winsome smile. "I have just received a shipment of lovely jewelry for Christmas. Would the hotel allow me to leave a small announcement on the counter for your customers?"

The middle-aged clerk enjoyed this small flirtation. He grinned, and, with an air of self-importance replied, " You just bring it by, little lady. We'll be more than glad to help."

"Thank you very much. It is so kind of you. And, while I'm here, may I make reservations for Thanksgiving dinner for my parents and myself?"

"I'll give you the best table in one of the front windows."

Elizabeth gave a demure look, "Thank you, sir. Is there a set time?"

"Anytime from one to five. You won't be disappointed."

"We'll be here at three."

She left the hotel with a feeling of accomplishment. Her parents had a room, Thanksgiving dinner was settled and she had a new outlet to advertise her shop. Perhaps she would leave a couple pieces of jewelry at the hotel as a sample of what she had to offer. Perhaps the jeweler up the street would not be one bit happy about that. Perhaps, she didn't care. Elizabeth needed the money for the days that lay ahead.

****

It was a bit after four o'clock on Wednesday afternoon when Elizabeth saw her parents enter the front door of her millinery shop. There was a sudden thud in her chest. She had rehearsed how she would greet them with a big smile and rush to tell them how happy she was to see them. But, that wasn't how she felt and she had learned to be true to her feelings.

Elizabeth gave them a tentative smile as she finished placing a hat in a hatbox before she came to meet them. "It's good to see you."

Her father, who had always been reticent about showing outward emotion, surprised her with a warm hug. "We have missed you, Lizzy."

Gertrude Fairchilds grimaced at the pet nickname. "We were glad to get here before dusk so you can show us around your shop," said her mother.

81

The awkward moment of their arrival had passed. "Do come in and sit down. I know it is a tiresome trip. Would you like some tea?" Elizabeth offered.

"A cup of tea would be welcome," her mother answered.

Elizabeth gave a faint smile. "I'm becoming an expert at brewing tea. If you'd like, why don't you browse around the shop? The kettle is already hot so it won't take long." She left without waiting for a reply.

In the back room, she was fussing with the tray, the teacups, and some scones she had made. Her parents talked in hushed voices. Were they pleased or disappointed? She had taken extra care to see all was spotless and the displays pleasing.

When Elizabeth moved into the shop, Catherine Burke had left behind three matching china cups and saucers decorated with tiny rosebuds. Most likely they were left because the fourth one had been broken. Rarely would there be use for a set of three. But, Elizabeth knew that china would impress her mother so she silently thanked Catherine Burke. When she returned with her tray of refreshments, her parents were seated in two delicate burgundy velvet chairs in the front of the shop.

Her parents were an odd looking pair. Francis Fairchilds was a short, slender, rather good-looking man in his mid forties, while his wife was a tall, plain woman with an ample figure. There were streaks of gray glistening in her dark brown hair as it pouffed out from under the outdated leghorn hat she always wore.

Francis Fairchilds rose when his daughther entered. "Here, Elizabeth, you sit here and I'll get one of the wooden chairs there by your work table."

"No thank you, father," she answered as she placed the tray on a side table. "I'll pull up the footstool. How was your trip?"

"Bumpy and uncomfortable. It was much more pleasant to come in the spring of the year," said her mother. "Now I hope we will find the bed in the hotel comfortable enough to sleep in."

"I wish I could offer to have you stay here, but as you know I only have the one bed upstairs."

"Which brings me to ask," said her mother, "how prosperous is the shop? I see that you have quite a few hats for sale and what is that jewelry?"

Elizabeth brightened at the mention of the jewelry. "Isn't it lovely? I was afraid I'd overbought, but it seems to be going well."

"It's cheap, Elizabeth."

Her mother's retorts could squelch an optimistic feeling quicker than squashing a bug. Elizabeth's face reddened.

"I believe what your mother means is that it's more inexpensive than what a jeweler sells." That was her father's attempt at softening the blow.

Elizabeth had promised herself she wouldn't get into a row with her mother. She swallowed hard before she replied. "I don't care to compete with a jeweler. They aren't genuine diamonds or emeralds or rubies but they are still tasteful. And, with all the help the government is giving our allies under this threat of war, people are not spending as freely." She turned and looked directly at her mother, "This isn't Washington, Mother, in case you haven't noticed." Then she yanked off the tea cozy. "More tea?"

At that moment, the door opened and in came Mary Lee Thompson. "Oh, I'm sorry, Miz' Elizabeth. I didn't know you had company."

"Come in Mary Lee. Mother and Father, this is Mary Lee Thompson. She works in the shop with me and, moreover, she is my friend. Mary Lee, these are my parents, Francis and Gertrude Fairchilds."

If Mary Lee was surprised, it didn't show. "I'm pleased to meet you."

"What brings you by?" asked Elizabeth.

Mary Lee gave a shy look. "I plumb forgot to ask you what you were doin' for Thanksgivin' when I was here on Saturday. Robert has invited me to go to his family's place down in Strasburg." She offered Elizabeth a basket she was carrying. "I made some molasses brown bread to take down and made an extra loaf for you."

Elizabeth took the basket from her and raised the lid. "It smells wonderful. I'm glad you will be going to meet Robert's family. Are you nervous?"

Mary Lee smiled, "I been jumpy as a cat."

"Would you care for a cup of tea?" Elizabeth asked.

"Oh, no thank you. I'd best be on my way. I got to finish sewin' the hem in my dress."

"A new dress? How wonderful."

"You know me better'n that. It's a hand-me-down but I fixed it up right nice."

"I can hardly wait to see it," Elizabeth answered.

Mary Lee giggled, "I'm plannin' on takin' it to Washington when we go."

Elizabeth heard her mother's cup hit the saucer.

"Well, I got to be goin'. It was nice to meet you both. Miz' Elizabeth don't talk much 'bout where she came from."

"I'm sure she doesn't," said Mrs. Fairchilds.

Mr. Fairchilds rose from his chair. "It was pleasant meeting you, Miss Thompson. I hope we will see each other again."

"It's Mrs. Thompson, Father."

He offered an apologetic nod.

No sooner was Mary Lee out the door before Elizabeth heard what she expected. "What ever do you mean that she is a friend of yours and that you are both going to Washington? She's beneath you, Elizabeth!"

"I don't think so. Mother, you must remember that I am a tainted woman. You said so yourself. Perhaps Mary Lee's English isn't up to perfection, but she is a true friend who cares about me." Elizabeth picked up the empty teacups. "Would you like to come up and see my apartment?"

"I certainly would," said her father as he picked up the tray.

Her mother remained seated, "If you haven't made some great changes, I'll just sit here and wait."

When they reached the apartment her father took her arm. "Elizabeth, we have both been worried about you. I don't know why your mother refuses to show it. It was her idea to come out for the holiday."

"Didn't she tell you about me coming to Alexandria to find out about the baby?"

With a shocked look, he answered, "No. Elizabeth you haven't been searching for the baby, have you?"

She led him to the kitchen. "Come and sit down, Father. I need to talk about this. I have found out that the baby was put in an orphanage, and I intend to find him."

She could see tears in his eyes. "Oh, my darling Elizabeth, when your mother and I made that decision, we felt it was the best we could do for you. You don't know how many times we've questioned our actions."

"Did you see the baby?"

"No, neither of us did. We just made the arrangements with a lawyer. He took care of everything. We signed over the rights of the parent because you were so ill that you needed someone to make the decision for you. We were given a temporary Power of Attorney."

She grabbed his arm. "Tell me the lawyer's name, Father. I have to find my child."

He patted her hand. "It will do no good. The agreement was made with your mother and me and it would be against a lawyer's ethics to divulge that information."

Elizabeth pleaded, "Just tell me his name, Father. That is all I'm asking."

"Do you want to come back and live with us in Alexandria? We can sell this place and you can return to where you rightfully belong. Forget about the baby."

Elizabeth sat back in her chair. "Now you sound like Mother. The baby is my own and he is your grandson, whether you want to claim him or not. I refuse to give up."

Her father gave a defeated sigh. "You always did have a stubborn streak and nothing I can say will stop that. I don't think it will do you any good, but he is a Washington lawyer by the name of Jacob Cunningham. That's the best I can do for you."

She ran and hugged him. "Oh father, you won't be sorry."

"Elizabeth, I believe this is all folly for you to even try. Now, come ahead and show me the rest of your apartment."

When they walked into the living room, he spied the tiny vase filled with dried flowers on her windowsill. "What's this, a spot of color to ward off the days of winter?"

Elizabeth picked up the crystal vase for him to admire. "That was given to me by a cavalry officer after we had ridden to Washington together on the train."

"A nice little memento. Is he from Washington?"

"No, he's from this area. He's on General Pershing's staff, I believe."

Her father shook his head. "Elizabeth, I'm afraid that our country is going to be drawn into this war in Europe, and, if we are, a lot of our boys aren't going to come back."

"Let's not think about that. Thank goodness, you're too old to go."

He laughed, "At forty-five I'm ready to sit with the women, huh?"

With an apologetic voice, she answered, "I didn't mean it like that." Then kissed him on the cheek.

"I know you didn't. Come now, I think we've left your mother long enough. She's probably building up to a boil and I shall be the recipient of her vexation."

Elizabeth laughed. "I'm glad we had this time to ourselves. I think we're going to have a wonderful Thanksgiving Day." Then on a somber note, "Do you think Mother will ever forgive me?"

Her father answered, "Forgiveness is a two-way street, Lizzy."

****

On Friday morning, Elizabeth bid her parents goodbye before they climbed into the twelve-passenger car that would take them up to the Bluemont Station.

The time with them had gone well. Gertrude's complaints were less than expected: 'the mashed potatoes are lumpy, the coffee is too strong, the beds at the hotel should be more comfortable, and the help are not trained'.

The cinema was playing a Mary Pickford movie, which filled in Wednesday evening and the three of them played cards in the hotel room on Thursday evening. Elizabeth did not mention Matthew to them again. She had the information she needed.

Herbert Marks was standing next to the twelve-passenger car that looked like a stretched out Model-T.

"Take good care of my parents, Mr. Marks."

"Miz' Elizabeth, You know you can trust me. I been makin' this run plenty of times." He went around the car and climbed into the driver's seat. Elizabeth watched as the noisy car took off with a jerk.

She waved as it putted down the street. It seemed this visit had brought the three Fairchilds closer together, but there was still a gulf of separation. Perhaps that is the way it is meant to be, thought Elizabeth.

Chapter 11

Christmas sales were brisk, which plumped up the money Elizabeth needed. She was packing for the trip to Washington that she and Mary Lee would begin the next morning. The train was to leave the Bluemont station at nine o'clock.

The hats Catherine Burke had sent allowed her the extra money she needed to buy both train tickets and pay for two nights at the Willard Hotel. As a gesture of gratitude, she and Mary Lee had picked out two items of jewelry for Catherine.

Mary Lee had fretted about Elizabeth spending Christmas Day alone. "It's just not right for you to be spendin' Christmas by yerself. Robert and me are goin'way down to Strasburg agin' but maybe I should stay here."

"That's very kind of you. Rest assured that I welcome the quiet time after the long hours we spent before Christmas. When we leave for Washington, I want everything back in order." She had handed her friend a small gift. "Here's your present. I want you to have it before you go."

It was then Elizabeth gave her the red pin with the little pearl dangling down that Mary Lee had admired from the first order of jewelry. When she saw what was in the package, she burst into tears.

"Miz' Elizabeth, yer too good to me."

"No, Mary Lee. You deserve more than this pin. I don't know how I could have gotten along without you."

They hugged each other and Mary Lee left the shop with an appreciative smile.

Now they would be going to Washington together. Elizabeth posted a notice in the front window of the shop that it would be closed until Friday, December 31st. That would allow them to return and open the shop for last minute buyers for New Year's Eve. According to Mary Lee, 'There's always them last minute people.'

Elizabeth was a bundle of energy. The excitement of going back to Washington was like a tonic and this time she would not have to go alone. They were to visit Catherine Burke's hat shop in Georgetown. Elizabeth's plan was to leave Mary Lee with Catherine for an afternoon. That would allow the time she needed to find the lawyer, Jacob Cunningham. No one had to know what her meeting was about. She was determined to get an answer to the whereabouts of her child.

Previously, Elizabeth had written to Catherine to thank her for the hats she had sent, and told her that Mary Lee would be coming to the city with her. Catherine had responded with a note saying she was overjoyed at the prospect of their visit, and she hoped they could spend a full day with her. That was when Elizabeth plotted out her course. She didn't look at it as being impolite to leave Mary Lee at Catherine's for a few hours because they had much to talk about. Besides, Mary Lee would help make a hat or two while she was there. She was not one to sit idle.

The next morning, Elizabeth was sitting in the foyer reviewing the list of what she needed to take with her when Mary Lee came to the door.

"I see Mr. Marks's big car is sittin' in front of the hotel. I'm not late am I?"

"No. Mr. Marks is probably in the Virginia House having his breakfast. The car leaves at seven-thirty."

Mary Lee was carrying a satchel and a small pocketbook. "Do you have everything you need?" asked Elizabeth.

"Most likely. I'll only need the clothes I have on, but I did pack another dress, my nightgown and my toothbrush and tooth powder."

Elizabeth smiled. She had packed a suitcase with two dresses, two blouses, a skirt, her nightgown, extra lisle stockings, another pair of shoes, a wool sweater and an assortment of toiletries. In a large tapestry bag she had: an umbrella, a book, writing paper, pencils, woolen shawl, Catherine's gift, and a bag of hard candies. She also carried a pocketbook with train tickets, an address book, money, handkerchief, and a small pillbox containing aspirin. "Mary Lee, I think you are the wiser of the two of us."

"My stomach has been flutterin' for two days. I'm so nervous about makin' this trip. I told Robert that maybe I shouldn't go an' he said that I'd be sorry if I didn't."

"We are going to have a good time. I suspect Robert will miss you enough that he'll propose the minute we get back."

Mary Lee blushed. "Wouldn't that be somethin'?" With a wide grin, she said, "If he does, I'd say, yes, and we could get married in June. That way people wouldn't be talkin'."

"Talking about what?" asked Elizabeth.

"Well, you know. If people get married too soon, everyone thinks they had to get married 'cause of bein' in the family way an' that kind of stuff."

"Some people get in the family way and don't get married," said Elizabeth with a sarcastic edge to her voice.

"Oh, but that wouldn't be right," answered Mary Lee.

"Perhaps not," said Elizabeth. "But, what do you think a woman should do if that happened? Give the baby away or keep it."

"I never thought much 'bout that, but if it was me, I know I'd go ahead and keep my baby. I lived through everyone snickerin' 'bout the way Zack was and makin' a fool of hisself, so I reckon I could live down havin' a baby without bein' married. After a while people ferget an' find somethin' else to gab about. How'd we get on talkin' about this anyway?"

"You were talking about getting married and people counting up on their fingers."

Mary Lee flushed, "Yeah, I guess it was me."

Elizabeth touched her hand, "I do value your opinion. It's time for us to leave. I'll put on my coat and hat and we can be on our way."

"Can I carry one of them bags fer you?"

"No thanks. I'll put my pocketbook inside this bag and then I can balance myself with the suitcase in the other hand."

"You do make me laugh, Miz' Elizabeth."

They went out onto the stoop where Elizabeth locked the door before she dropped the key into her bag. She was happy to leave the shop, the apartment, and the town.

Herbert Marks was out loading traveling bags into the long car when Mary lee and Elizabeth arrived. "Goin' back to the city, Miss Fairchilds?"

"Yes, and Mrs. Thompson is going with me. We'll be looking for you on our return trip on Thursday."

He picked up her suitcase while he held the door open for the young ladies. "Goin' to take in the sights, huh?"

"We hope to," answered Elizabeth.

Mary Lee offered, "We're goin' to visit Miz' Catherine while we're there."

Herbert gave a big smile. "You tell her that I send my regards. We all miss Miz' Catherine." And then, with a slight apology, "Not that we ain't happy to have you here," Miz' Fairchilds."

Probably as happy to have me here, as I am to be here thought Elizabeth. But, she gave him a sweet smile and said, "Thank you, Mr. Marks."

Elizabeth made her way to the back of the twelve-passenger car and Mary Lee followed. Elizabeth sat first so she could place her satchel on the floor to the left of her feet. She leaned over and whispered to Mary Lee, "I like to sit in the back so I can watch everyone else get on. Has your stomach stopped fluttering?"

"Not yet. I sure hope it does when we get to the train."

"We'll have a stop over in Leesburg where we can get something to eat. I was so excited about this trip, I didn't have breakfast."

"Maybe by then my stomach will be lookin' for food. I couldn't eat anythin' last night or this mornin'," Mary Lee confessed.

"Do you want a hard candy to suck on? I've got some in my bag."

"Is it peppermint?"

Elizabeth answered, as she reached for her bag, "Some of them are. I'll fish one out for you."

Herbert Marks got the passengers' attention. "Everybody ready? Hold onto your hats. We're about to head for the mountain."

A couple of the passengers chuckled. Elizabeth felt Mary Lee stiffen next to her. "Here's the peppermint. It's a clear day so we'll have a pleasant ride up to Bluemont. I'm so pleased you decided to come," said Elizabeth.

"I'll either be glad or scared outta' my wits," whispered Mary Lee. "I ain't never done nothin' like this before."

"No, and you may never do it again. But isn't it exhilarating?"

"Whatever that means," said Mary Lee.

Chapter 12

Tuesday morning, Elizabeth and Mary Lee sat side by side on the trolley taking them to Georgetown. Mary Lee had been in awe since they left the Bluemont Train Depot yesterday.

"I swear Miz' Elizabeth, I'm gonna' have a stiff neck from lookin' at all this wonder. I never saw such big, tall buildins'. An' people...why, they're all dressed up and look so important." She sat next to the trolley window with her nose pressed to the glass.

Elizabeth addressed her in a quiet tone, "Don't you think you should start calling me Elizabeth?"

Mary Lee was wide-eyed. "I thought we done settled that."

"I don't want people to think you're my servant instead of my friend. Besides, you're older than I am."

Mary Lee smiled, "Well, that's true. But, if there's one thing I know in this life, it's where I fit and you'll always be Miz' Elizabeth to me. Don't mean we cain't be friends."

Elizabeth gave the young woman's hand a friendly squeeze. "Where did you learn all of this worldly lore?"

"It wasn't hard. Other people are quick to let you know yer place."

Elizabeth changed the subject. "I'm sure you and Mrs. Burke will have a lot of catching up to do. I have an errand here in Washington. Will it be all right if I leave for a few hours in the afternoon?"

Mary Lee was unruffled. "That won't bother me and I'm sure Miz' Catherine will be fine with it."

"I'll be as quick as I can, but I do have rather an urgent matter to attend."

The conductor stopped by their seat. "You ladies will want to get off at the next stop," he said.

"Thank you." Elizabeth responded. "I understand there will be a trolley back to Washington at five o'clock. Is that correct?"

"Every hour on the hour until nine in the evening," he answered and continued to the back of the car.

The young ladies enjoyed the two-block walk to Catherine's house from the trolley stop. It was a pleasant day for December so they unbuttoned their coats to let the air breeze through as they walked.

The Burke house was a two story, red brick, federal-style house that sat about a hundred feet from the road with a walk leading up to the portico. The Georgetown Millinery sat to the left, nearer to the street.

Before they came to the steps the door opened and Catherine came running out to meet them, her long honey-brown hair parted in the middle and pulled back in a bun. There was sheer joy in her hazel eyes as she flew down the steps and grabbed Mary Lee with a warm hug. "I'm so glad you've come," she said. "You don't know how wonderful it is to see a familiar face."

"I'm happy I got here," replied Mary Lee. "I'm not sure I'll ever do it agin'."

Catherine was beaming. "And, Miss Fairchilds. How nice to see you again. Come inside. Mattie has prepared a little snack for us before lunchtime." She entwined her arms in theirs as they mounted the short set of steps.

Inside the foyer, a large colored woman who appeared to be as strong as an ox met them. She took their coats.

"This is Mattie. She helps me here at the house. Mattie this is Miss Fairchilds and my friend, Mary Lee. She was my helper in my shop before I moved here."

"Yessum," she said, and nodded her head in the young ladies' direction.

Catherine motioned toward another room. "Let's go into the parlor and you can tell me about your trip."

The parlor held a settee with two matching chairs in the French style, where the two young ladies took a seat.

Catherine said, "I wanted to bring my chintz living room set, but Patrick said this furniture was an heirloom to be passed down. I find it as stiff as some of the French people I've met. I was sorry to leave the chintz in Berryville, but it was a small concession to make for my husband."

Elizabeth laughed. "I understand, but I'm very happy you left the furniture. I can just fold up on the sofa and drift off to sleep."

Catherine gave a wistful look. "Mary Lee, remember when I had that terrible case of the grippe and I could hardly get off the sofa?"

"Don't remind me of that, Miz' Catherine. I thought you might be a goner fer sure."

Mattie wheeled in the teacart at that moment. She had arranged delicate hand made pastries on a silver tray giving a silent statement to her contribution in the Burke house.

"Oh, Mattie," Elizabeth exclaimed. "How exquisite. I wish you were helping at my place."

Mattie's expression never changed as to whether or not she was pleased with Elizabeth's compliment. She wheeled the cart to the side of Catherine's chair before leaving the room.

"If you can come by tomorrow evening for supper, you can taste Mattie's chicken and dumplings. I've invited our friends, the Thomases, to dine with us. Patrick will be home early and we don't get that opportunity too often. Since he's gone back to medical school, he's away a good deal of the time. You know Carolyn, Mary Lee. When I told her you would be in town, she said she would delighted to see you."

"I would like to see her. Will she bring the baby? She had such a bad time before the baby was born, it was good to see them both okay. What do you think, Miz' Elizabeth?" asked Mary Lee.

"I think it would be a very nice evening. Tonight we are attending a concert at Constitution Hall and tomorrow we are going to the Smithsonian. It would be good to have a casual evening before we have to leave the next morning."

"I'll be plumb wore out when we get back home. Miz' Elizabeth keeps me goin'. I don't think there's anythin' she cain't do. She even reads tealeaves," Mary Lee announced.

Elizabeth blushed. "It's mostly in fun."

Mary Lee wasn't deterred. "She's right good at it. Miz' Catherine, You should let her read yers."

"Mary Lee, I'm sure Mrs. Burke does not want me to read her tealeaves."

"Oh, but I do," said Catherine. "I think it sounds like a grand idea. I used to try it, but it never worked out. How do we go about it?"

As Elizabeth explained the process, Mary Lee beamed with pride. After they finished the tea, Catherine did as she was directed.

Elizabeth studied the cup carefully. When she was satisfied with her observation, she said, " The hats are in there, many of them. I believe you will have enough business for quite some time. And, over here it looks like a light of some kind."

"That's probably the light I leave on for Patrick. He spends lots of hours up at the hospital."

"And, my goodness," exclaimed Elizabeth. "I'm not sure exactly what this means. Has anyone in your family recently had a baby?"

Catherine raised her eyebrows and gave a light-hearted reply, "Not in my family. Carolyn's like a sister. It must be her Ann Catherine. But that was six months ago. These must be old tealeaves."

They all giggled.

Elizabeth continued, "No, it wouldn't be a friend. There's a cradle in here and it would have to be someone in the family."

"The only other person it could be would be my sister-in-law, Sarah."

Mary Lee grinned from ear to ear. "What about you, Miz' Catherine? Maybe it's you."

"That's not likely, Mary Lee. I'm almost twenty-seven."

"That don't mean anythin'. Minnie Alphin was married for a long time and finally had a baby when she was close to forty."

Catherine laughed. "Mary Lee, you do have a way of putting things into perspective."

"There, see what I mean, Miz' Elizabeth? Miz' Catherine is good at them big words, too."

When tea was over, Catherine gave them a tour of the house before they walked to the hat shop. Rex, Catherine's dog, followed them and took his rightful place in front of the warm fireplace inside the shop.

The large work area was quaint. Wooden pegs held hats in various stages of finishing. Elizabeth spied a tall, navy-blue, porcelain vase decorated with a picture of The Hunt both front and back.

"What a beautiful vase," Elizabeth remarked.

"Actual pictures of the Blue Ridge Hunt," Catherine responded. "Whenever I feel a bit melancholy, I look at the pictures on the vase and it soothes my homesickness."

Mary Lee was busy examining every nook and cranny of the millinery shop. "Miz' Catherine, I think I could stay here forever," Mary Lee said.

"I do like my shop. Do you recall that I asked you to come and work with me?" Catherine asked, bringing her musing back to the present. "I've asked Mattie to serve our lunch out here at two."

"I remember you askin' and I was glad you did, but I got somethin' to tell you."

This was an opportunity for Elizabeth. "May I call you, Catherine?"

"I believe we should all be on a first name basis. Thank you, Elizabeth, for breaking the ice."

"I have some business to take care of in the city while Mary Lee fills you in on what has been going on in her life. Would you mind if I leave? I can be back at two, I'm sure."

"Of course I wouldn't mind. Mary Lee and I will catch up on the news in Berryville."

"I do apologize, but there is an urgent matter that I must attend to."

And to allay the concerned look of Mary Lee, Elizabeth added, "It's not serious, but it does need my attention. By two o'clock I will be more than ready for lunch." She turned at the door. "While I'm gone, Mary Lee can tell you all the good news."

Elizabeth left the millinery shop and hurried to the trolley as she had five minutes before she would have to wait another hour. It would take thirty minutes to get to the lawyer's office.

She was anxious about seeing Jacob Cunningham. Even though her father had only given her his name, it hadn't been difficult to track him down. She looked him up in the phone registry. Elizabeth was determined to get the information she needed about her son and he would have to give it to her. He would just have to!

Chapter 13

The next evening after a day at the Smithsonian, Mary Lee and Elizabeth were to be at Catherine's house for supper. Mary Lee had worn her new dress to last evening's concert and deemed it appropriate to wear to the Burkes'. Elizabeth agreed. It was a soft teal, a perfect color for Mary Lee's red hair and pale coloring. A darker shade of chenille trimmed the three-tiered skirt. Elizabeth wore a satin cream blouse, maroon skirt and an embroidered vest trimmed in white fur and a matching turban of maroon with a thin band of the same fur.

"Miz' Elizabeth, you are just too pretty for words. Are you goin' to be able to get on and off the trolley in that tight skirt?"

"It's called a hobble skirt. I'll just hobble on and off."

Mary Lee was pinning on her plain black felt hat. "I surely hope so," she said.

"Is Mrs. Thomas the lady who has the baby?" Elizabeth asked.

"Uh-huh. Haven't you met Miz' Carolyn?"

"No. The week Catherine stayed to help me in the shop, I remember her saying she had to go visit Carolyn, but I was too wrapped up in my own problems to pay attention to anything."

"I don't know Captain Thomas all that well but he must be pretty nice if Miz' Carolyn married him."

They put on their long coats and picked up their pocketbooks before leaving the hotel room.

Elizabeth turned to lock the door. "I hope it isn't going to be an uncomfortable evening."

The remark took Mary Lee by surprise. "Do you 'spect so? I don't like to feel stuffy. Caint' we just eat and leave?"

"That wouldn't be polite."

She hooked her arm through Mary Lee's as they went down the hall of the hotel and out the front door of the Willard to walk to the trolley.

Elizabeth asked, "How did Catherine look to you?"

"She looks real happy. I think Mattie's cookin' has added some fullness to her, but she's still the nice Miz' Catherine. We had such a grand time talkin' together yesterday. I think we got caught up on everybody in Berryville. She even said that once in a while she'd like to look out her window and see Miz' Talley waddling across the street. But not too often, mind you."

Elizabeth gave a knowing smile. "We can all get homesick. Married life must agree with her. That was the reason she moved to Washington wasn't it?"

"That was the only reason," Mary Lee answered. "She fell hard when Mr. Patrick showed up."

They began to cross the street. "You still haven't told me why you came out to Berryville. It must have been hard to leave all of this behind."

"More difficult than you know," Elizabeth answered. "We'll discuss that another time because right now we have to hurry. We can't miss the trolley. It's important to get to the Burkes' on time. It wouldn't do to keep them waiting."

The four o'clock trolley was crowded so Mary Lee and Elizabeth had to make their way to the back seat. Elizabeth was almost sorry she had worn the tight skirt but it was all the fashion. Passengers took an extra look at the comely miss as she shuffled by.

When they reached Catherine's house, Mattie answered the door. "Miz' Burke is in the parlor. I'll take your coats."

"Thank you Mattie," they said in unison, and then giggled like schoolgirls. Mattie just shook her head as she walked away to take care of their coats.

By this time, Catherine was out of the parlor with Carolyn close behind carrying her little one.

"We are so happy that you could come," said Catherine as she took their hands in each of hers. "Mary Lee you remember Carolyn."

"Oh, Miz' Carolyn, it's so good to see you. Everyone asks me if I hear about Doctor Hawthorne's nurse. Now I can say I done seen you. And look how pretty your little one is." Mary Lee let the baby wrap her hand around her finger. "She's got yer dark eyes, Miz' Carolyn."

The proud mother beamed. "She's a good baby, not that we didn't have some colicky times."

"Miz Catherine, yer new necklace looks right nice."

Catherine held it out for all to see. "This was a gift from Elizabeth," Catherine advised. She has a line of jewelry in the shop. And, it is past time for you two to be introduced."

"Carolyn, this is Miss Elizabeth Fairchilds. Miss Fairchilds, meet my good friend, Carolyn Thomas."

Elizabeth stepped forward, "Mrs. Thomas. How very nice to meet you. I know Mary Lee holds you both in high regard."

"Please call me Carolyn because I intend to call you Elizabeth. I feel old enough, as it is, juggling this little one around. Children have a tendency to make one feel their age."

Elizabeth was captivated. "She's beautiful."

"I wanted to name her after Catherine, but she said that was too confusing, so we gave her that middle name and call her Annie."

"Ladies come into the parlor where we can almost be comfortable," said Catherine. "The men are enjoying a smoke and a glass of wine in the library. It's really the den but it was the only place to put all of Patrick's books so we call it the library."

The young ladies went into the parlor where Mary Lee and Elizabeth chose the settee, once again, and the others sat in the side chairs.

"Mattie will have supper ready in about ten minutes. I suggested we have some tea and tidbits when you arrived, but she said she didn't want anything to interfere with eating her food, 'not after all that work I'm gonna' have to do.' I knew better than to insist."

Elizabeth had hardly taken her eyes off Ann Catherine. "Do you think the baby will allow me to hold her?" she asked Carolyn.

"She's starting into that finicky stage but let's see how it goes? She's getting a bit heavy to carry around." Carolyn rose and placed the baby in Elizabeth's lap. She waited until her child was comfortable before returning to her chair. The baby never let out a cry of protest. "She certainly takes to you, Elizabeth."

Elizabeth forgot the other ladies in the room as she happily kissed the baby's hands, touched her nose and played pat-a-cake with her charge until Mattie announced the food was ready.

Elizabeth handed the baby back to Carolyn before following Catherine and Mary Lee into the dining room. Catherine was dressed in a plaid taffeta skirt with a high collared, forest green waist. Carolyn was in a simple but elegant cream lace dress. Both outfits were tasteful but neither the high fashion of the day.

Elizabeth wondered if they thought she was overdressed. Goodness knows she had no occasion to wear this outfit in Berryville The odor of food from the kitchen broke into her thoughts and made her realize how hungry she was.

Catherine announced their seating arrangements as the men came into the dining room.

Elizabeth was introduced to Patrick and Asa. "We might as well take our seats, the Major will be along in a minute," said Patrick. The men seated the guests and then their wives.

Elizabeth and Mary Lee met each other's eyes with a worried look. Catherine had not said there would be another guest

"Don't eat without me," came a voice from the hall. "I'm famished."

Patrick answered, "Come right in. You'll be seated between our guests."

Elizabeth was so startled to see Andrew Caldwell enter the dining room she almost tipped over a glass of water.

"Major Caldwell, may I present Miss Elizabeth Fairchilds and Mrs. Mary Lee Thompson," said Patrick as Andrew came into the room.

"What a delightful surprise," said Andrew and nodded in acknowledgement. "Ah, Patrick, these are two lovely lasses with whom I am acquainted."

Elizabeth and Mary Lee turned crimson before Elizabeth found her voice, "Good evening, Major Caldwell. I believe we met when you were a captain."

"Asa and I have moved up in rank. But, I'm still as charming as ever," he grinned, and took his seat.

His arm brushed hers, which sent a tingle to her toes, instantly quashing her appetite.

Throughout the meal, Elizabeth said little using the time to study the other people present.

She had taken an instant liking to the warmth of Catherine. Patrick had a gentle way about him and a surprising quick wit. To Elizabeth they seemed to be a well-matched couple.

Between Asa and Carolyn, she sensed deep passion. Asa's brawny build, military bearing, and dark brooding eyes commanded attention. Yet, his adoration of his wife and child was evident. Carolyn, on the other hand, was animated and outspoken when it came to politics and the Women's Movement. She was fully entrenched in both; praising Wyoming for putting a woman in congress, and lamenting the fact that President Wilson was not in favor of giving women the right to vote.

"Once Ann Catherine begins to walk, she'll have her in one of those white uniforms marching through the streets of Washington," quipped Asa.

Carolyn playfully tapped him on the shoulder and kissed his cheek. "I understand, it's time for me to change the subject."

This outward display of affection was foreign to Elizabeth, but deep down it gave her a good feeling.

"Andrew, how does it feel to be a major?" asked Patrick.

"The pay is better." That brought a smile to everyone's face. "I have a few more responsibilities. Asa's in the same boat, but I think we are both well pleased with our appointments."

Andrew turned his attention to Elizabeth. "What about you, Elizabeth? Are you enjoying your time here?"

111

"Mary Lee and I couldn't have had a better time. We've been to the Smithsonian, taken in a concert at Constitution Hall, and visited every monument we could find." She gave Andrew a thankful smile for including her in the conversation.

Mary Lee chimed in, "Land sakes, not only that but I think we walked in and out of all the stores in the city. I might have to buy a new pair of shoes when we get home."

And that brought a big laugh from everyone.

"Well, I am very glad you came to visit," said Catherine.

Mattie appeared at the door. "I done got apple pie and tea set up in the parlor."

"Thank you, Mattie," answered Catherine. "Let's adjourn to the parlor. You haven't tasted anything that can compare to Mattie's apple pie."

In the parlor, Andrew chose a seat next to Elizabeth. She was beginning to feel a certain level of comfort having him close and it was disconcerting to her. It was plain to see why he was favored by the ladies. He had an easy and likeable manner making one feel special.

When it was time to leave, Andrew offered to see them back to the hotel in a cab. Elizabeth declined. "That's kind of you, but we have purchased our return trolley tickets."

He gave her that disarming smile, "That's of little consequence. The cab will be faster and with me taking care of the fare, it is a bargain."

That seemed to please Mary Lee. "What do you say, Miz' Elizabeth? Gettin' in a car will be easier than you hobblin' into the trolley."

That sentence stopped whatever conversation was going on with the others in the room. At least they were polite enough not to laugh aloud.

Elizabeth rolled her eyes. "Mary Lee, I'm sure Major Caldwell has to get back to his base. We will have to hurry to get the last trolley."

"Tonight's a late night," advised Andrew. "I don't have to be back at the base until midnight."

What else could she do to save face but to agree. "Then, I assume taking a cab is a better choice."

They said their thank you and goodbye before Andrew and the young ladies walked to the Model T Ford taxi that waited at the side of the street.

Andrew gave the driver instructions as he helped the two young ladies into the back of the cab. All three sat together with Elizabeth in the middle. She was pressed so close to Andrew that she felt smothered. It was becoming an inner fight to not let him affect her. Tomorrow she would be back in Berryville, where she knew that it would be good for her to be seventy miles away from Major Andrew Caldwell.

Chapter 14

Mary Lee lay awake in the narrow bed in the hotel room. She was so excited about the prospect of returning home that she couldn't sleep. She could hear the rhythmic breathing of Elizabeth in the other bed but was unsure if she was awake. In the stillness of the night she let her mind wander.

She mulled over the evening they had spent. It was good to see Miz' Catherine happy and acquaint herself with Miz' Carolyn and her little one. The way Major Caldwell gave Eizabeth admiring glances all evening gave Mary Lee some concern. Of course, if he is the ladies' man that people say he is, maybe that's the way he treats all the pretty young ladies of his class, she thought. It wouldn't do for Miz' Elizabeth to get hurt.

This visit to Washington had been more than Mary Lee had ever thought. Elizabeth seemed to be right at home. Mary Lee felt overwhelmed. She knew where she belonged and the city wasn't the place. It made her realize how comfortable she felt in her way of life. And, then there was Robert. She missed him more than she had expected, and she could hardly wait to get back to see him. Maybe Elizabeth was right. Maybe Robert would miss her just as much and maybe he would ask her to marry him. That was a lot of maybes. But if he did, Mary Lee knew that she would say yes.

Robert was everything she wanted in a man. All of these thoughts were too much to think about so she turned on her side and prayed to get some rest.

A voice from the darkness whispered, "Mary Lee are you asleep?"

She whispered back, "No, I'm wound up like an eight-day clock."

Elizabeth turned on the bedside lamp and sat up. "So am I. I wish we had a cup of tea."

"What do you suppose it is? Maybe somethin' in Mattie's cookin'?"

Her friend let out a long sigh. "I don't think it's that simple. We both have too much going on in our lives and the dark of night makes it all pop out in our minds."

"I 'spect yer right. Were you surprised to see Major Caldwell?"

"Surprised and perplexed," Elizabeth answered.

Whatever that means, thought Mary Lee. "I'll sure be glad to get home."

"It's been a good trip. But, for the first time, I can say it will be good to get back to work in the shop." Elizabeth settled herself back under the covers. "Let's try to get what sleep we can." She turned off the light and fought back tears as she envisioned her baby in a crib in some bleak orphanage completely unaware he had a mother who longed to hold him.

****

The last time Andrew checked the clock it was one o'clock in the morning. His eyes were wide open staring at the dingy white ceiling. His mind kept playing over this evening. Miss Elizabeth Fairchilds had gotten under his skin and he didn't like the feeling.

She had been cordial enough, but there was no indication that she either enjoyed his company or cared to see him again. He wasn't used to that kind of treatment from young ladies in which he took an interest. It was true there had been many. To his knowledge he had never sullied a girl's reputation, and he didn't consider himself any different from a lot of young men he knew who appreciated the company of the ladies.

But, Andrew was now twenty-five and no longer the young carefree man of five years ago. Life was easy until his friend Asa met Carolyn. He and Asa were like brothers with a lighthearted approach to life. Asa had been the one to keep Andrew on the straight path, but now his responsibilities lay with Carolyn and their baby daughter. Andrew sat up on the side of his cot still hashing over the evening's events. He left the cot to pour a glass of water. The light from the street lamp gave his room a dull glow as he stood looking out the window sipping the water. There was enough of the moon to cast an eerie light on the heavy mist of the December night. All at once an overpowering feeling of loneliness crept into his being. The hollow sensation in his gut was unlike him, and for the first time Andrew could remember, he was lonely.

Was Elizabeth feeling the same way? Why couldn't he get her off his mind? She was clearly a young lady of careful breeding, yet she was running a hat shop and keeping company with a woman beneath her station in life. Something had to have happened and he was determined to find out what it was. Perhaps some young man had spurned her charms and set her against men altogether. But that wasn't likely. Young love is fleeting and people move on. No, there had to be something in her background keeping her in a cloud of secrecy.

Carolyn was right. Andrew Caldwell was smitten. It was clear to him that he wasn't going to be able to sleep so he got dressed. Perhaps a brisk walk in the early morning hours would wash away his unsettled mind. He slammed the door on his way out oblivious to the fact it may have awakened others in the house.

Chapter 15

Robert met Mary Lee and Elizabeth when they arrived in Berryville the afternoon of December 3o[th]. It allowed Mary Lee and Robert a day together, and it gave Elizabeth time to recover from the trip, straighten the shop and hope for a good sales day on Friday.

And, that is exactly what happened. As predicted, ladies who needed last minute items for a New Year's Eve celebration made a steady stream of buyers. Elizabeth was elated. It would take money to do the investigating she needed to do to find her little one.

Jacob Cunningham, the Washington lawyer she had visited, while leaving Mary Lee with Catherine, was of some help. He had said, "I'm sorry but, even if I could open the file with your parents consent, you will find that all has been turned over to the Catholic Church." Which Elizabeth concluded meant her little Matthew was in a Catholic orphanage. The lawyer also advised that the baby had been approved for adoption to an influential family in Washington.

Time was not on her side.

****

On New Year's Eve, Robert proposed to Mary Lee. She had come to the hat shop on New Year's Day with an excitement that Elizabeth

118

envied. Mary Lee wore a small diamond ring Robert had bought at the jeweler's while the young ladies were in Washington. "I am so happy for you. Have you set a date for the wedding?" Elizabeth asked.

"We talked about June, but there ain't no day picked."

Elizabeth put her fingers to her lips and contemplated. "Six months, a proper engagement period, and it will give us time to make plans. Oh, Mary Lee, this is the most wonderful news I've had in ages." Then she stopped. "I'm sorry. I jumped right in as though I were going to help and didn't give a thought to your wishes."

"Right now, everythin's all up in the air. If you want to help me, I'd be most happy. I ain't too good at the plannin' part."

A week later on Sunday, Robert and Mary Lee invited Elizabeth to go roller-skating at the rink in Winchester. She had no interest in roller-skating, but she wanted to go to the library and do some research. She had seen a picture of a huge building in the *Winchester Star* newspaper called the Handley Library. Perhaps she could find information about Catholic orphanages.

Sunday turned out to be a clear, sunny day. Robert came by early with the carriage and Elizabeth came hustling across the street as he was driving up. Mary Lee was bundled up in the middle of the seat and Elizabeth climbed in beside her.

"I hope you brought a warm blanket," Mary Lee said. "That air is right cool."

"I did," replied Elizabeth. "I have this heavy, wool shawl to lay across my lap."

Robert smiled at them. "You ladies didn't 'spect me to come ready? I got a big raccoon robe tucked in the back."

Mary Lee wrinkled her nose. "I'll bet it stinks."

"Only when it gets wet," came his smug reply.

Robert tapped the horse with reins and they started off. Lavinia was still at church services, so for once, they escaped her ever-observing eye.

"I have some food in the basket we can eat on the way home," Elizabeth remarked.

"Good," Mary Lee answered. "What did you pack?"

"Some roast beef sandwiches and oatmeal cookies."

"I brought hard boiled eggs and fried chicken," said Mary Lee.

Robert joined the conversation. "I got a jug of cider in the back. We can wash it all down with that."

"It better not be hard," Mary Lee teased.

"Just a bit of a buzz to keep us warm," he teased back.

The young ladies giggled.

When they reached Winchester, Robert stopped in front of the Handley Library. It was a majestic building in the heart of town.

"The roller rink is a couple blocks down that way. We should be headin' back around four," said Robert. "Would you like for us to pick you up here?"

"I'll walk over to the roller rink. Have fun skating." Elizabeth stood and waved as they drove off.

She went up the steep set of steps and through the heavy oak doors with leaded glass windows that opened into the main library. Polished marble floors glistened under the massive central dome. She found her way to the card catalog and started her search under orphanages, where she found little information. Then she went to Roman Catholic. That wasn't much help unless you wanted information on the early church.

She must have looked puzzled for the librarian came by and asked if she needed assistance.

Elizabeth told her what she was searching for.

The librarian paused before she answered. "We have a Catholic church here in town. Perhaps they would be more apt to have the information."

This was news to Elizabeth. "How do I find it?"

"When you go back down the front steps turn left. The next street up is Loudoun Street. Go south on Loudoun for a few blocks. The church is on that street."

Elizabeth thanked her and set out with haste.

Following the directions she was given, she found the Sacred Heart Church. A sign said,

Rectory, so she walked up to the door and was reticent to ring the bell. What was she going to say? Who was she going to meet? What if it was a priest and he was mean, as some of the girls at school had said? But, she was here and she had to make the attempt. With her heart in her throat, she swallowed hard and closed her eyes as she rang the doorbell.

To her surprise a middle-aged lady answered her ring.

"Yes, Miss. Can I help you?"

"I need to talk with a priest," Elizabeth blurted out.

"This is Father's quiet afternoon. Is it something I can help you with or can it wait until tomorrow?"

Elizabeth felt her throat tightening. "Oh no. I won't be in town tomorrow. I have to see him today."

Before the housekeeper could respond, a short, gray-haired, kindly looking man appeared at her side. "It's fine, Fanny. I'll see the young lady. Come in, Miss…"

"Fairchilds," came her quick reply.

"Come in and have a seat. I'm Father Quinn, the pastor here at Sacred Heart."

Elizabeth followed him into a small office and took a seat opposite him. Her heart was beating like a hammer.

"Now, what is it that couldn't wait?" he asked, as he calmly took his seat in a well-worn easy chair. Elizabeth sat on the edge of the straight chair. How should she begin? How was she going to tell him the reason she was there unless she gave the full story? Her mind was mulling over the words while he waited patiently. There was nothing to do but to tell the whole sordid tale. Once she got started, after little stutters and clearing of her throat, she was surprised how easily the story slipped out.

It felt good to tell it to someone. She had kept it bottled up for so long. When she finished, if Father Quinn was shocked, he didn't give any indication. He just sat for a quiet minute.

"That's a heavy burden you have been carrying around. We are all human and we all make mistakes. I find it admirable that you have the desire to get your son. It won't be easy for you, if you do manage to find him. You are a young woman on your own, and from what you've told me, he has a good family waiting to adopt him."

"I have given that much thought. But I have to persevere until I come to the end of the road, wherever that may lead."

The priest sat for a moment in thoughtful repose. "I can give you the names and addresses of the three closest homes in and around the Washington area."

Elizabeth felt a flood of relief by his words.

"As I recall, there is one in Washington, one near Baltimore and a home in Richmond."

He rummaged around in a pile of papers strewn about his small desk.

Then he searched the cubbyholes in the desk. Finally, as if the thought had just struck him, he reached into a cabinet and took out a large book.

123

"Ah, here we are. I'll jot these addresses down for you."

When he finished and handed it to her, Elizabeth was overjoyed. She wanted to give him a great hug, but that wouldn't be proper, so she grasped his hand and thanked him with all her heart.

"I hope you are successful," he said. "I have found the nuns who run these places sometimes rule with an iron hand. If you come into an impasse, we shall try again. It helps to have a priest on your side when it comes to the good sisters. Are you of the faith, Miss Fairchilds?"

"Oh, no. I'm an Episcopalian."

He smiled, "Well, last I knew that was within the Christian fold."

Elizabeth felt her face turn crimson, but it didn't deter her exuberant feeling. She was aglow with her good fortune, and tripped on down the street with a light air.

She walked over to the skating rink a few blocks away and watched Robert and Mary Lee skate two more rounds.

Mary Lee's face was bright pink from the energy of skating, and Robert was wiping his brow with a large handkerchief.

"Miz' Elizabeth, that must have been a good day at the library. I swear you look bright as a polished copper pot."

Elizabeth beamed. "It's surprising what kind of information you can get at the library. I've had an exhilarating day."

"Whatever that means," mumbled Mary Lee as she unlaced her skates.

****

It was the middle of February and two weeks since Elizabeth had sent inquiring letters to the three orphanages. She had heard nothing. Surely, she had expected at least one of them to reply. But they hadn't. Maybe her letters were read and just tossed in a wastebasket. Perhaps she should send another letter in case the first ones didn't arrive. Maybe she should go back up to Winchester to talk with Father Quinn again.

After mulling over all the maybes and perhaps in her mind, she resigned herself to patience for another week before she did anything further.

A couple days later, Lloyd Pierce came by with the mail. Elizabeth wanted to grab it out of his hand. "How are you doin' today, Miz' Elizabeth? It's a chilly one out there today."

"I'm fine, thank you for asking. Do you have any interesting mail for me?" She was sure he checked all the return addresses.

"Now, what would you call interestin'?" he teased. "Maybe this one with Major Caldwell's name on it?"

She flushed a bright red.

"I assume he's the same Andrew Caldwell that used to be a captain. Must have moved up in rank," he said, as he handed the letter to her with that knowing little smile on his face.

"Major Caldwell was at supper at the Burke's house when Mrs. Thompson and I visited. Perhaps it's related to that." Why was she feeling he needed an explanation? He was only the postman. Then it struck her that his next stop would be Lavinia's. Any slip of the tongue could have untold consequences.

"You're not going to tell Mrs. Talley, I hope."

"Now, Miz' Elizabeth, I hope you know me better 'n' that. I just like to tease a little like I used to do with Miz' Catherine."

"I am sorry. It is a curious piece of mail."

"I'll say it is. See you tomorra'."

Once Lloyd Pierce was out the door, Elizabeth zipped open the envelope with her silver letter opener .It was a valentine with a picture of an attractive young lady wearing a hat. On the front it read, *Roses are red, violets are blue,* inside, it continued, *and, that's how I feel when I'm not with you.*

Below the inscription was his note:

Dear Elizabeth,

Do you like the saucy hat this captivating lady is wearing? Her blonde curls and flashing eyes remind me of you. I will drop by your shop next week when I am in town.

I trust that all is well with you.

Sincerely, Andrew

Her first impression was that he had pluck to send the card, and then to compound it by saying he will be stopping by the shop. He didn't ask, he just announced. Well, it was a public place of business; there was no reason he couldn't stop in. Maybe he would buy something.

Elizabeth sat there rereading the card when Mary Lee came through the door. She came to where Elizabeth was sitting as she unbuttoned her coat. It was a large card so Mary Lee's eyes were drawn to it. "My, that's a right pretty card with all the lace, flowers and hearts on it. I 'spect its a valentine."

"You 'spect right," answered Elizabeth, still chagrined at the audacity of Andrew. "Guess who sent it."

"That's not hard, unless you got other admirers I don't know about. I'd say it's from Major Caldwell."

"You're right. How did you know?"

"Now, Miz' Elizabeth. He couldn't hardly take his eyes off you when we went to Miz' Catherine's house. I cain't believe you didn't see that."

Elizabeth smiled, remembering the evening. "To be honest, I was too busy trying not to look at him. He's going to be in town next week and he's going to come by. I think that's too bold of him."

Mary Lee grinned. She took a seat at the work counter and picked up a hat in the trimming process. "You know that old sayin', "Faint heart ne'er won fair lady.""

"Where did you hear that?"

127

"Mr. Pierce. He used to like to tease Miz' Catherine."

"Mary Lee, I am flattered with Major Caldwell's attention, but I cannot let myself get involved with a man."

"Any man or just Major Caldwell?" She wrinkled her forehead.

"Any man."

"It's not my place to say, but you lead a pretty lonesome life. It sometimes worries me you keep so much to yerself."

Elizabeth gave a plaintive sigh. "Sometimes it worries me, too. But, I am determined to make enough money in this shop that I can sell it and move back to the city. I can't let a man get in the way."

"Maybe not. But life don't always work the way you want it to." She held the unfinished hat on her hand. "What do you think if I make a bow out of this cream colored ribbon and stick this yellow bauble right in the middle?"

Elizabeth pictured what Mary Lee described. "That would be attractive."

"You know what would be even prettier?" asked Mary Lee. "That pin with the yellow stone that's got the three strands of tiny pearls dangling down from it." She got up, hat in hand, went over and picked the pin from the jewelry display. " Look at this, Miz' Elizabeth, I could just slap that in there and some lady will pay twice the price."

Elizabeth smiled "Mary Lee, you are going to outwit me in the merchandizing department."

Mary Lee looked tentative. "I guess that's good?"

"That's outstanding. Let's have some tea and I want to read your tealeaves."

"Why ever do you want to do that?"

"Because," answered Elizabeth, "I want to be sure you're still going to work with me after Robert makes you his bride."

"Don't remind me of that. It makes my knees rubbery just to think on it."

Elizabeth took her by the arm, "Then let's not think about you getting married or me having to deal with Major Caldwell. Let's just enjoy a hot cup of tea."

Chapter 16

When Friday afternoon rolled around and there was no sign of Andrew, Elizabeth wasn't sure how she felt: relieved, disappointed, or irritated. Mary Lee had gone home in the early afternoon because Robert was taking her to the cinema that evening. Elizabeth had only one more hour before she could put the closed sign in the shop window.

As she was boxing up a pair of gloves for a waiting customer, she heard the tinkle of the shop bell. Glancing up she felt a ripple of anticipation as Andrew entered. Her mind went fuzzy causing a slight tremor in her hands as she closed the lid of the box. "You picked out a lovely pair of gloves. They will complement many different outfits."

The customer responded, "I am pleased. I plan to return when I have more time to try the jewelry."

"Please do. I have some lovely pieces coming in for the spring and summer seasons. The jewelry was popular for Christmas."

"I have no doubt that it was. Thank you Miss Fairchilds. I shall return to see the new selection."

"You are welcome. I look forward to seeing you," came Elizabeth's reply.

Andrew held his cap in his hands and flashed a smile at the lady as he opened the door for her to exit. Elizabeth stood watching this display of chivalry. The woman gave a demure smile and fluttered out the door. Did Major Caldwell affect all women the same way?

The short interlude gave Elizabeth time to gather her senses. Assuming a nonchalant air, she began to clear off her work counter. "Hello, Andrew. I received your card, but it didn't give the time when you would be arriving."

He came a few steps into the room. " I wasn't sure, myself. From the information we're receiving this will most likely be the last furlough I will get for some time."

Elizabeth stopped and looked at him. "What do you mean?" she asked.

"May I sit down?"

"Of course. How impolite of me not to offer you a seat. Would you care for a glass of water or a cup of tea?"

"No thank you," he said, " but good of you to ask." He pulled a chair over to the counter where she was doing her best to look busy.

He sat while Elizabeth fussed about the counter before taking her seat to face him.

Andrew was his usual relaxed self. "This is a bit awkward, isn't it? You behind the counter and me leaning over to talk to you." He flashed her a wide grin and she felt the heat rush to her face.

Her emotions were swirling like an eddy in a pool. "It's a safe distance," she answered. "You didn't answer my question. What do you mean when you said this might be the last furlough you'll be getting? Do you have news about the war? We're all deathly afraid we'll be dragged into it."

"Asa and I get bits and pieces of what goes on in the higher command. They are discussing how the war in Europe is going and they may need our help with troops."

Talk of war had been going on for months, but, for the first time, Elizabeth was alarmed at the possibility. "President Wilson wouldn't want that, would he?"

"No one wants war. Sometimes it can't be avoided." He sat back in his chair for a pensive few moments. "Would you spend the weekend with me?"

Her surprised response was immediate, "What an improper suggestion! Exactly what do you have in mind, Major Caldwell?"

"Nothing illicit, although that would be nice," he teased.

She became indignant, "Whether you are testing me or teasing me, I don't appreciate it."

Andrew didn't move and gave her a benevolent smile. "Now see? You didn't wait to hear what I meant by my proposition. If this is to be the last time I will be able to spend time with you, I would very much like to have your company while I am here. I'd be pleased to have you come and visit at Red Gate Farm. There is plenty of room. There are also plenty of chaperones. It would give this cavalryman much pleasure before he gets shipped off to God knows where."

Elizabeth's short flare of temper had dissolved, replaced by a touch of sadness. What if the country did go into war, and what if Andrew and his friend were shipped to a foreign land? Asa had a wife and child. What would become of them? And, God forbid, what if either Andrew or Asa were wounded or worse yet, never returned home? All of these thoughts flipped through her mind.

If Andrew wished to have her chaperoned company for the two days, what harm could it do? Just cause a big flurry of gossip. She was sure it wouldn't stop ladies from buying in her shop, and she wasn't going to live in this town forever, and it would get her out of a lonely weekend. Without further hesitation, she rationalized herself right into agreeing.

"I can't promise that Mary Lee can tend the shop tomorrow. I wouldn't be free until after five in the afternoon."

Her words put a spark of life into Andrew. "Where is Mary Lee? I can go find her and ask if she can help you out."

"I imagine she's at her house. She and Robert are going to the cinema this evening."

"That's Jim Dandy," Andrew said as he popped out of his seat. "Let's go to the cinema and we can ask her there."

That caused Elizabeth to pause. "I'm not sure that's a good idea."

"Are you concerned that people will talk if they see us together?"

Elizabeth gave a wry smile, "Now, you know they will talk, Andrew. I'm sure Mrs. Talley spied you coming in here and will have her nose pressed to the window to see when you leave. Up to now I haven't given any reason for gossip. I hope to keep a clean slate."

"It will be purely on the up and up. What's the harm in going to the cinema? I will be on my best behavior." He was like a little boy hoping to get the prize lollipop in the bunch. "I'll stay at the hotel overnight and we can leave early in the morning."

Elizabeth was wary. "We haven't even asked Mary Lee." Then reality struck. "Mrs. Talley will blow it out of proportion." She shook her head. "No, on second thought, I'd better not risk it."

"Bosh to Mrs. Talley. We can leave by your back door and she'll never be the wiser."

So Andrew was aware there was a back entrance. That was a surprise. "How did you know I had a back door?"

"Just a guess. Every place has another way to get out."

The whole idea was intoxicating, and she could do with some zip in her life. "I know Mary Lee won't say anything. Do you think it's possible?"

"We won't know until we try," he answered.

They met eye to eye. "I'm game," she said. "You reserve your room, and pick me up for the cinema at six-thirty."

It became Andrew's turn to doubt. "What if Mary Lee can't watch the shop?"

Elizabeth smiled "Well then, I'll just have to close the shop for the day."

"You would do that for me?" he asked in pleasant surprise.

"No, I would do that for me," she answered, pleased with her self-confident attitude.

She walked Andrew to the door where she turned the closed sign and locked the door behind him.

Upstairs, she sat for a few minutes to clear her swirling thoughts. Her eyes caught the small crystal vase of dried flowers that Andrew had given her and it brought a smile to her face. She would do her best to enjoy this weekend. It seemed it had been so long since she had experienced carefree days that she was determined to tuck her troubles away. They would surface quickly enough when she returned. Not knowing what to expect gave her some consternation, but Andrew was a fun-loving sort and easy-going and had made it sound as though he would be her constant companion. She would deal with the periphery, as it presented.

When they arrived at the cinema, most seats were taken. Andrew asked a young man if he would move over one space so there would be two seats together. The young man obliged with some reluctance until Elizabeth gave him an enticing smile. He seemed more than willing to have the pretty young lady seated next to him.

Once seated, Elizabeth began to peer around to see if she could spot Mary Lee. It was Robert she spied first. "There they are over to the left about four rows up," she whispered into Andrew's ear.

"I thought so when I spotted two heads of red hair."

Elizabeth stifled a giggle.

He settled back into the seat. "We'll catch up with them at the intermission. Do you know what's playing?"

She shook her head.

"It'll be a surprise to both of us," he said as the lights dimmed.

Elizabeth was delighted when the title flashed across the screen. "The Fireman" with Charlie Chaplin. Everyone clapped.

Midway through the film there was a fifteen-minute intermission, and the projectionist abruptly turned off the machine.

Andrew escorted Elizabeth out into the small lobby where they waited to see Mary Lee. When she and Robert arrived, her mouth dropped. "Miz' Elizabeth, whatever are you doin' here?"

"I came with Major Caldwell," she replied, which Mary Lee could plainly see.

Andrew acknowledged both of them before drawing Robert off to one side. "We'll get some refreshments," he said. Robert was quick to do Andrew's bidding leaving the young ladies together.

"I have to ask you a big favor," Elizabeth whispered. "Come over here and have a seat where we aren't in the midst of everybody."

They went to sit at the far wall trying not to step in the popcorn that people were freely dropping on the floor.

"Wouldn't you think they would be more careful instead of tryin' to shove a handful in their mouths?" Mary Lee said in disgust.

Elizabeth paid no attention. She had a more important matter. Once out of earshot of others, Elizabeth asked, "Can you watch the shop for me tomorrow? Andrew has invited me to spend the weekend at his family's farm and I intend to go."

Mary Lee was taken aback. "That cain't be right. I mean...do you think you should?"

"There will be his family there. He's going to meet me out back tomorrow morning so Lavinia won't see us."

"But, Miz' Elizabeth. There's goin' to be talk. And you know that ole' Miz' Talley is goin' to find out one way or another. Just comin' with him tonight is goin' to be big news."

"Mary Lee, I have got to get away from that shop or I'll go out of my mind."

Her friend kept her voice confidential. "But, he's known as a ladies' man. It just won't look right yer goin' over there fer two days."

"I'm going to close up the shop if you can't help me out."

Mary Lee gave a deep sigh. "Well, I 'spect if your mind's made up then I cain't change it. I'll watch the shop, but don't blame me if stories get blabbed all over town."

"As I said before, his family will be there."

137

"Uh-huh," said Mary Lee.

Elizabeth covered her friend's hand with her own. "This is the last visit Andrew is going to have for a long time. Perhaps I'm not using my head, but I would really like to spend the time with him."

"Whatever happened to, 'I cain't let a man in my life'?" Mary Lee asked in a deflated tone.

"It's only for two days. By Monday, Major Caldwell will return to his post and I will return to the drudge of the hat shop."

"And, that will be the end of it," Mary Lee replied with an all-knowing look.

"Of course," said Elizabeth.

"Of course," echoed Mary Lee.

Chapter 17

Somehow Andrew had arranged for a car to take them to Red Gate Farm. Elizabeth didn't ask, she was just happy to go. As planned, they had left by the back door after Mary Lee showed up to watch the shop.

After an hour of jostling along dirt roads and bouncing up and down from ruts left by heavy wagons, they arrived at Red Gate Farm. The red brick manor house sat on a rise overlooking the countryside, although in February the scenery was dull to Elizabeth's thinking. The driver left the vehicle and opened a large red gate that gave the farm its name. In what Elizabeth considered a thoughtful gesture, Andrew drove the car through to save the man the inconvenience of getting in and out of the auto. The driver closed the gate and resumed his rightful seat behind the wheel. He drove up the tree-lined drive, where the majestic oaks were bereft of leaves, and stopped at the flight of limestone steps that led to the covered porch spanning the front of the huge stately house. Andrew paid the driver and carried Elizabeth's bag up the steps.

To her surprise there was no one there to greet them. "Did you tell them we were coming?" she asked.

"Yes, in a way. I sent a letter that I may be coming and that I may be bringing a guest."

"A letter saying that you may be coming?"

"Because if I said I was coming and bringing a lady-friend, curious eyes would be making you uncomfortable."

"My mother would have been horrified if I had brought a guest when she didn't expect it. Or, worse yet, if she had made preparations and then I didn't show up."

"Elizabeth, we have hired help that keep this house spotless and a wonderful cook in the kitchen, who is always prepared, although she might sputter a bit."

Andrew opened the door and took her coat. As if by magic, a maid appeared. "I'll take your lady's coat, Mistah' Andrew."

"Thank you, Diane. This is Miss Fairchilds. She will be spending the weekend with us."

The maid gave a nod to Elizabeth and a sideways smile to Andrew.

Did he bring young ladies here often?

"This will be your room," he said, as he opened a heavy oak door. "Carolyn used this room when she took care of mother."

"Carolyn?"

"Yes, Asa's wife, Carolyn Thomas. She's a nurse. Don't you remember? You met her at the Burkes'."

"I guess I wasn't thinking. Of course I remember. I held her beautiful child."

They entered the room where he placed her bag on a side table.

"I wasn't aware she was a nurse."

"Carolyn was a Godsend. Mother suffered from an illness we would like to put behind us. She met Asa here when we came for a Harvest Weekend."

Elizabeth unpinned her hat. "I would like to get to know Carolyn," she said as she ran her fingers though her blonde hair. "She was quite knowledgeable about the suffragette movement, and, her little Ann Catherine is so lovable I could hug her all day."

Andrew opened the curtains to let in the noonday sun. "I'm not sure Asa is thrilled about Carolyn's interest in the women's movement, but he is still a man very much in love. I suspect he will allow her that transgression." He turned to look at Elizabeth.

She stood with hands on hips, "So, the women's rights movement is a transgression in your eyes?"

He gave a sheepish look, "Poor choice of words," he admitted.

"Poor choice, indeed!" was her heated response.

He was not apologetic. "I have nothing against it, but sometimes Carolyn can get carried away. I think what Asa objects to is the white uniform and seeing his wife marching through the streets of Washington."

"I may concede him that point. But, I do believe women get trampled in this man's world. I will do my best to lend support."

"You promise to not march in the street," he said. "I promise I won't trample over you."

She couldn't help but smile.

"Now, I'll leave you to freshen up and if there is anything you need, just ring that bell on the desk. Diane won't come running, but she will get here as soon as her round body will allow."

He opened the door to leave. "I'll warn Mother we're here and come back in about twenty minutes. Is that reasonable?"

"Do you think she will be upset? I'm beginning to feel that I shouldn't have come. It was an impetuous decision."

"It was the right decision. Mother will be delighted. Besides, I did send that letter. Twenty minutes?"

"I'll be ready," she answered.

Once he had gone, Elizabeth took the liberty of surveying the room and was pleased with what she saw. A cherry four-poster bed with matching dresser, an upholstered settee, and lady's cherry desk. It was a comfortable room. A fire in the small fireplace would have been welcome because the room was a bit chilly. Perhaps she should ring that little bell and have someone come running. Having the luxury of being waited on, once again, was tempting, but she wasn't there to play the role of a haughty guest. Elizabeth stood looking out the window and drank in the warmth of the noonday sun with her mind not registering the country scene before her. Had she made a mistake in coming? Andrew, true to his word, had been the perfect gentleman, but would his behavior change as they spent more time together? It was too late to worry about that now.

Elizabeth freshened up and was ready when Andrew arrived twenty minutes later. She wore a patterned satin waist and gray felt skirt. Andrew had changed from his uniform into a white turtleneck sweater and black pants.

Mrs. Caldwell sat in the parlor, where she was reading. "Mother, I'd like you to meet my friend, Elizabeth Fairchilds."

Andrew had been right when he said that he favored his mother. She had the same auburn hair, green eyes and lithe build.

Virginia Caldwell rose from her chair and came to give Elizabeth a warm handclasp. There was no evidence of surprise that her son's guest was a young lady. "I am pleased to meet you, Miss Fairchilds. Come in and sit down. Andrew's father is out checking on the stock so we have some time to chat. Lunchtime will be soon and Mr. Caldwell never misses that."

Andrew led Elizabeth to a comfortable armchair facing his mother, while he sat on a love-seat.

"Where is everyone?" he asked. "I thought they would be around on Saturday."

"Will is out with your father, and I assume that Emily is in her quarters. God only knows where Ruth is. I wish the girl would get married so someone could keep tabs on her."

"She's hardly a girl, mother. She's twenty-three," replied Andrew with irritation. "You and father have spoiled her so that she won't find any man who satisfies her."

Elizabeth interjected, "I have met Ruth, Mrs. Caldwell. I own the hat shop in Berryville and she has been a good customer."

"Thank you, dear. How insensitive of us to forget that we have a guest in the room. Andrew and I frequently have a difference of opinion when we talk of Ruth. I believe she is a source of embarrassment to him."

Andrew rolled his eyes toward the ceiling.

"Tell me about your hat shop."

Elizabeth moved a bit trying to relieve the stiffness she felt. "It's a small place, something my parents thought would allow me to be self-sufficient."

"I see, and has it proved to be that?"

"I am satisfied. My plans are to make it profitable so that I can sell it and return to the city."

Andrew sprang upright on the settee.

Mrs. Caldwell answered, "Perhaps I would agree if I were born and raised in city life. I applaud you for this undertaking. It must have been difficult for you to settle into town."

Elizabeth took an instant liking to Andrew's mother.

"I have to be honest and say that it has not been an easy adjustment. But, I have had the friendship of Mary Lee Thompson. She is a sweet person whom I can trust with anything, not to mention the talents she brings to making hats. I have to admit my shortcomings in that department."

Virginia Caldwell smiled at their weekend guest. "I am so pleased that Andrew has invited you here. We will have a feast for supper where you can meet the rest of our family. I'm sure Andrew has plans for this afternoon."

He rose from his chair and kissed his mother on the forehead. "I plan to take Elizabeth around the farm."

"But you must have lunch."

"I'll have Ollie pack us something."

"Andrew, don't be ridiculous. It's February, hardly the time to go on a picnic."

He leaned down beside his mother's chair to be at eye level. "What ever happened to your spirit of adventure?" he teased.

His mother patted his hand, "Well, then go." She told him in playful disgust.

Then she looked over and gave Elizabeth a reflective smile. "He's all yours, Miss Fairchilds."

"Are you ready, Elizabeth?" he asked in a lighthearted manner and offered his arm.

"I believe I am in for an interesting after-noon," she responded.

"That I can promise," came his reply.

"Your father still insists dinner at six so keep that in mind," his mother called as they were leaving the room.

Andrew took Elizabeth down a back stairway that led to the kitchen. He put his finger to his lips

145

to make a quiet entrance. A kettle was whistling so the slim, little black lady bustling about the stove didn't hear them come in. Andrew sneaked over and tapped her on the shoulder, which caused her to jump and let out a cry. He was quick to stay her arm so he didn't get clobbered with the wooden masher she held in her hand. Andrew picked up the startled woman and whirled her around.

"Hello, Ollie," he said, before letting her down and giving her a warm hug.

"Mistah' Andrew. You are goin' to be the death o'me yet. I wasn't tol' you was comin' home. Now I gots one more mouth to feed."

"Two mouths, " he corrected, and motioned Elizabeth to come over from the foot of the stairs where she stood.

"Ollie, I'd like you to meet, Miss Fairchilds. She is to be our guest until tomorrow."

"Wal' chile' you are jus' the purtiest thing I ever seen. I don' know how you can put up with the likes o'him…scarin' me out of my skin like that. Shameful, that's what he is."

Shameful. It was the exact word her mother had leveled at her. The difference was that Ollie's was in fun. Her mother's had been degrading.

"Ollie, I'd like to have you put something together for me and Elizabeth to take in the carriage. Toby is bringing it around and we won't be back until suppertime."

"Jus' come runnin' down here and 'spect me to get you some food together jus' like that?"

she snapped her fingers. "Wal' I s'pose I can fin' somethin' aroun' here."

In five minutes they were on their way with a basket of food and a jug of water.

A short, burly, black man was standing by the carriage. He tipped his cap to Elizabeth and handed the reins to Andrew. "I done tossed a heavy quilt in there so the young lady can bundle up. It might get right chilly before you get back."

"Thank you, Toby."

" Good to have you home, Mistah' Andrew."

"It's good to be home," he replied as he tapped the horse with the reins.

"Your hired help seems to be fond of you," Elizabeth commented.

"Ollie and Toby have been a part of my life since I was born. They've been married for over forty years."

"So they live here?"

"Got a nice little house down the side road. I'll point it out as we get along."

There were numerous tenant houses on the estate. Andrew showed his favorite places: riding trails, a stone outcropping that housed a spring, and his favorite spots to sit and sort out his thoughts.

Elizabeth found it peaceful. "It's no wonder you want to come visit as often as you can."

Pointing up to a spot that held a large flat rock, he asked, "Do you want to take a chance and have lunch on that rock? We can spread out the quilt."

147

"I am hungry," she answered. "A climb up the hill will do me good."

Ollie had packed egg salad sandwiches, a couple of chunks of cheese and two pieces of small spice cakes. They washed them down with ice-cold water from the jug causing Elizabeth to shiver.

"Are you cold?" Andrew asked with concern. "Perhaps I had better get you back to the house."

"It was just the shock of the water. I'm in no hurry to return." She looked off into the distance. "I find it so restful here. In the city I used to go to my room for solace, but this is like a whole world of comfort. You are fortunate, Andrew."

"Yes, I am. Not only for the beauty of this place," he hesitated before he continued, " but also because I have met you, although you are a puzzle to me."

"And, why is that?"

"I have known many young ladies, and I'm not being boastful when I say this, but after a couple of meetings they are currying my favor. Do you like me at all, Elizabeth? Because, if you don't, I'm going to try to stop hoping you do."

His words caught her off guard. She was careful with her reply. "Of course I like you Andrew. Otherwise I wouldn't have consented to be here. I came with you this weekend for two reasons: one, because I wanted to be in your company, and two, because I would go mad if I was cooped up in that apartment one more lonely weekend. I suppose it was selfish on my part. If it seems I'm keeping my distance, it is because there is a matter in my life I must remedy. There is nothing that can get in the way."

He reached for her hand. "We'll keep it on a friendship basis. But, if your circumstances change, I'd like to be the first one to know." His impish grin made her smile.

She squeezed his hand, "I promise you will be, but it isn't likely," she answered.

"Your hands are freezing," he said. "Let's get you wrapped up in the quilt and head for warmer pastures."

Andrew seemed satisfied. Elizabeth let out a sigh of relief. Now they had a mutual understanding and she would do her best to make the rest of her visit enjoyable for both of them.

When she returned to her room in the mansion, she found a lively fire in the stone fireplace. Rather than remove her long wool coat she stood and absorbed the heat until she felt the warmth in her body return. She lay on the bed and covered up with a down quilt. Andrew would come by a few minutes before dinner so she allowed herself an hour to rest and enjoy the luxury of being waited on. She didn't have to cook the meal, wash the dishes or sweep the floor. It was a glorious feeling.

Dinner was promptly at six o'clock. Elizabeth was introduced to Andrew's father, William, before she met the rest of the family. They consisted of his short and blustery brother, Will, Will's quiet, demure wife, Emily, his sister, Ruth, whom Elizabeth had met, and his mother.

"Our granddaughter is away at finishing school," advised William. "We are happy to have you with us, Miss Fairchilds."

"Please call me Elizabeth."

"Would you care for a glass of wine?"

How polite but also unfair to be the first one offered. She would love to have a glass of wine, but it would not be proper if the other ladies did not. She smiled at the kind gentleman. "Thank you, but no, sir."

The wine bottle was emptied as all filled their glass except Emily. Out of the corner of her eye, Elizabeth had seen Will turn his wife's wineglass upside down. Strange, she thought.

The conversation at the table dealt with horses and farm matters. They inquired of Andrew about Asa and Carolyn and he proudly passed around a picture of them holding Ann Catherine.

Ruth was the one who couldn't resist. "I am really surprised you've met Elizabeth, Andrew. It's not like you to shop the millinery. Word must have gotten around about a new young lady in town."

She turned her attention to Elizabeth. "Andrew has been known to court the ladies."

He was seated next to Elizabeth and she felt him stiffen.

Ruth was not going to get the best of her. "And, what charming man hasn't? I'm sure the ladies did not shy away from his attention."

William Caldwell cleared his throat. "I'll ring for dessert."

The conversation returned to the affairs of the estate.

When dinner was over, Andrew led Elizabeth to a large upstairs ballroom.

"The floor is still scuffed from the Harvest Weekend."

She was in awe of the lovely room. A few scattered chairs were placed about and a crystal chandelier hung from the ceiling. She guessed it to be three-feet wide.

"What a grand room. It must be a sight with couples swirling around."

"Would you care to dance? We have some waltz records in that Victrola over there."

She looked in the direction he pointed. "Oh, Andrew, could we? I haven't danced in so long."

"Come on. I'll crank the old girl up and lets have a go at it. If we had different records, we could do the turkey trot. That's all the rage."

They broke between dances to select another waltz and after the fifth round of dancing Andrew said, "If we dance anymore, we'll have to play the same ones over."

"I'll be bushed tomorrow. You are a divine dance partner, and I should know because I've had to endure many partners."

He lifted the record from the turntable. "We're a good pair, Elizabeth. Keep that in mind."

He didn't have to tell her. She had drifted around the floor like a feather in his arms. Had she ever been so contented?

The next morning she awoke after a restful night's sleep. It was only she and Andrew for breakfast in the dining room. "Do you ride?" He asked.

"I used to."

"I thought we could go for a ride around the place before I have to get you back to town."

"I'd like that but I don't have any riding clothes."

"Mother must have some old ones around here someplace. I'd recommend borrowing some from Ruth, but you can tell we are not on the best of terms."

Andrew's mother had a wool riding skirt and jacket in a chest. They smelled of mothballs and were wrinkled but they would do for a ride on a crisp winter day. With the pungent smell of the mothballs, she was sure Andrew would keep his distance. They almost overpowered her. He came to her door with his mother's riding hat and held his nose as he handed it to her.

"You don't have to say anything, Andrew, I know I smell. It's your idea to go for a ride."

He backed into the hall. "Follow me," he ordered and they set off in the direction of the stables.

Once outside they could both breathe easier.

In the stable were two horses saddled. "You'll be riding Ginger. She's gentle but has enough spirit if you feel the urge."

He helped her into the saddle before he sprung into his.

152

"Are you ready?"

"As ready as I'll ever be."

Off they went at a slower pace until Elizabeth signaled that she felt comfortable on the horse. Then Andrew called to her saying he was going to go on ahead because he wanted to exercise his mount. He pointed in the direction he was going. "I'll wait down by the stream."

Elizabeth watched as he raced off. Watching Andrew galloping away gave her a rush of excitement. She spurred her horse and Ginger responded with spirit. She flew after Andrew and was on his heels when they came to an abrupt stop at the stream.

"I thought you said you hadn't ridden in years."

"I don't know what got into me. I saw you charging ahead and I couldn't hold back."

"Could it be there is competition in your make-up?"

She answered with a satisfied smile.

They dismounted and let the horses drink.

Elizabeth stretched her body. "I'll be sore tomorrow."

"I have to say I was impressed with your ability."

She sat on a fallen log as the horses drank. "Andrew, I'm so happy I came. These two days have been rejuvenating. Thank you so much for inviting me."

He lowered himself to sit next to her. "Believe me, the pleasure is all mine. I don't look

153

forward to going back. We'll be seventy miles apart. You'll be here and I'll be in Washington."

She gave a wistful sigh. "I think that works well," was her reply.

"In other words, you want me out of reach."

She touched his arm. "It has nothing to do with you and everything to do with me." Tears were welling up and she couldn't let him see. Elizabeth raised herself from the log and went to the horses.

Andrew came to her side. "Can I be of help?"

She could only shake her head.

"Are you sure?"

She nodded.

He gathered the reins of the horses, and helped her into the saddle.

It was a quiet ride back to the stables.

Chapter 18

In the morning, Mr. Caldwell's driver drove Elizabeth and Andrew back to Berryville. Andrew was to return to Washington on the two o'clock train. The driver parked at the back gate behind Elizabeth's shop. Andrew handed him some money. "Why don't you go to the Virginia House and have a meal? I have half an hour before we have to leave."

"Yes, sir," said the pleased driver. "I'll just leave the car here and be back by one-thirty."

Andrew took Elizabeth's bag and opened the latch on the heavy wooden gate.

"I believe we might get some snow," he surmised as they hurried across the fenced backyard.

The town run had ice on it. They walked over the small footbridge and up to the back porch. Elizabeth took her key from her pocketbook and handed it to Andrew. He unlocked the door and they went up the back flight of stairs.

"I'll get your fire started before I leave," he said. "Do you have plenty of dry firewood in case we get a cold spell?"

"That's one thing I've learned. Once, I was caught without dry wood and thought I would never get warm. I guess we learn by our mistakes." Those were words to live by. She smiled to herself. "I'll heat up some milk for cocoa, and, if you'd like you can go straight down this hall and get a fire stared in the living room fireplace."

He did as she suggested and returned to the kitchen.

"A nice place you have here. I noticed you kept the small vase of dried flowers. I guess you like them."

"I can't recall if I ever thanked you, but I like them very much. The flowers have been a bright spot during this long winter."

She took two mugs from the cupboard. "I must tell you, Andrew, that after we ate together at the Willard, I didn't think I would ever see you again."

"Perhaps I'm like the bad penny that always turns up."

He took a seat at the kitchen table. "Elizabeth, I want you to know how much it has meant to me to have spent these couple of days together."

She warmed the mugs, poured the hot cocoa into them and sat them on the table. Ollie had made them lunch before they left Red Gate. "Would you like a cookie to go with that?"

"No thanks, the cocoa will be enough, I'm stuffed. Ollie always outdoes herself when I come home."

Elizabeth took a seat opposite Andrew. "We did have a good time, didn't we? I loved dancing to the records on the Victrola, and taking the horses on that romp through the fields. It was cold but invigorating."

She gave a pensive look," Sometimes, I get so lonely here, I could just curl up and die."

"You don't have to stay holed up here. Anytime you need a change, my parents would love to have you come visit at the farm. Mother liked the fact that you enjoy playing chess, unusual for a young lady. Even Ruth was civil to you, except for the snide remark about you running a hat shop."

"Ruth wouldn't be Ruth unless she tried to make someone feel inferior," said Elizabeth. She took a sip of the warm cocoa. "If you are sure your parents would be open to me visiting once in a while, I would very much like to."

"You may have to put up with Will and Emily. What did you think of them?"

Should she be honest? Of course she should. "I found Will pompous and overbearing and Emily too timid."

Andrew smiled, "Wouldn't you be if you were married to Will?"

Like a flying dart, it struck Elizabeth that she could very easily have fallen into that type of relationship if she had married Edward. Didn't he possess that same pompous attitude, and wasn't she too naive to realize it? It caused her mind to drift away from what Andrew was saying.

"I'm sorry, Andrew. I was in another world. What were you saying?"

"I was saying that I hope whatever is keeping you preoccupied gets resolved."

She laughed. "I hope you're right. What if I told you I once thought of getting married?"

His answer was immediate. "Is that supposed to shock me? It doesn't surprise me one iota that you would be found a desirable spouse. What happened?"

"Let's just say, it was a big mistake."

"Turn you off men, did it?"

"According to my mother, it turned men off me."

He reached across the table and took her hand. "You have been deeply hurt. I'm sorry."

She gave a tentative smile. "Andrew, I don't know what got into me. I didn't mean to dampen the afterglow of our lovely two days together." She glanced at the clock. "And look at the time. You only have ten minutes before you have to leave."

He still held her hand. "Time with you is always pleasant even if it is to discuss some failings in your life. It gives me a better understanding. Would you care to hear about some of mine?"

Elizabeth laughed and slipped her hand from beneath his warm and sensitive touch. "I don't believe I would."

He sat for a moment. "Elizabeth Fairchilds, may I kiss you?" he asked.

This was unexpected. "We are to keep our relationship on a friendly basis. Isn't that what you agreed to?"

"What's more friendly than a kiss?"

She slowly shook her head. "I don't think that's a good idea."

He smiled. "You haven't answered my question."

"One kiss can lead to shaky ground."

He was not to be deterred. "I may be shipped away. Wouldn't you feel guilty about denying a soldier his last wish before he goes to defend his country?"

She laughed aloud. "From what? We aren't at war."

His hangdog expression tugged at her heart. "Okay," she acquiesced. "One kiss for a man who may be off to who knows where. Make it short and sweet."

"It will be short, my sweet, because a lingering kiss would send me to my knees." He cupped her face in his hands and their lips gently met.

"That wasn't so difficult was it? I shall keep that in my memory," he said as he brushed his finger across her cheek.

Elizabeth understood why Andrew Caldwell was popular with the young ladies. He was irre-sistible.

Andrew went around the table to retrieve his jacket off the back of the chair he had been occupying. "Let's not wait for a shipping away to write to each other," he said. "I will send you letters and expect an answer for each in return."

"It would certainly break up the boredom of the long days in the hat shop."

"You promise to write?"

"I promise to write."

"Good. Now I have to run."

159

With a touch of sadness, she watched from her kitchen window as the car carrying Andrew pulled away from the back gate. All she had left was the quiet and loneliness of her upstairs apartment. She knew he was as attracted to her as she was to him. If he knew the truth about her, would her mother's words prove true: 'no decent you now'?

****

Andrew was at the small Bluemont train station with a few minutes to spare. He purchased his ticket and waited on the platform to board the coach. The quaint town was still, unlike the bustle of the spring and summer months.

The conductor hopped off the car and placed a step stool to aid the passengers in boarding. "Good afternoon, sir," he addressed Andrew. "Nice to have you with us again. Hope you had a favorable weekend."

"Most favorable," answered Andrew. "Good of you to ask."

There were plenty of empty seats but he made his way to the back. Back to the very seat where he'd had the unexpected pleasure of sitting next to Elizabeth. He smiled at the memory of her trying to act nonchalant. It was their second unexpected meeting and she had been aloof both times. Because of her indifference, he had been cautious; a new role for a man who'd had his pick of young ladies eager for his attention. He smiled to himself as he recalled the weekend.

He relaxed in his seat and went over the events of these past two days. It gave him much pleasure to recall the sweetness of Elizabeth. She had promised to write and he would have to be content with that for now. He would bide his time and hope to win her over. Perhaps he didn't have much time, the thought of war seemed ever present and it was a constant battle to push it out of his mind. For a man whose wants had always been fulfilled, Andrew found himself in a state of unrest. Was he finally growing up?

Chapter 19

Elizabeth had written letters to three orphanages inquiring about her little one. She had heard nothing. Should she write again? Perhaps it would be wise to go to Winchester and talk with the priest who had been so helpful. Every day that went by made the discovery of Matthew Quinton Fairchilds whereabouts more doubtful. She wondered what he looked like. Does he have blond hair like mine? Is he beginning to walk? Can he say any words? Most of all, is he being cared for with love?

This was March. At the end of April he would be a year old and eligible for adoption. According to the lawyer, children from a Catholic orphanage had to be a year old before they could be adopted. That seemed a strange rule but it did give her a window of hope.

She sat at her work counter trying to decide what her next step should be when Lloyd Pierce, as if by the hand of Providence, came barging in the door with a heavy sack of mail. "I swear Miz' Elizabeth, this mail pouch gets heavier every day. Got a few for you. Couple of them look interestin'."

"Mr. Pierce, you do keep an eye on the mail."

"Only way I can stay ahead of Miz' Talley," he said, as he placed the packet of mail on the counter.

"I see most of your jewelry is gone. Gonna' order any more?"

"It should be coming in any day now. I'm surprised you ask. I don't recall your coming in to buy that lovely necklace Mrs. Pierce fancied." She cocked her head and gave him a sly smile.

"I just let it fly out of my mind, and, don't you know I got the what for. I figure I'll have to make it up to her."

Elizabeth moved the packet of mail aside. "The spring and summer lines are most attractive. Perhaps, she'll find one even prettier than the one that got away."

He shifted his mail pouch to the other shoulder. "I 'spect so. I gotta' be off to drop Miz' Talley's mail. She's got a couple of small packages in here. Probably some of those ugly bird statues she keeps collectin'. Loads down my sack."

Elizabeth gave him a playful smile. "Helps you keep your job," she said.

"Now, Miz' Elizabeth, whose side are you on?"

"I'll see you tomorrow, Mr. Pierce. Give my regards to Mrs. Talley," she called, as he was leaving.

Elizabeth opened the bundle of mail to find a fashion magazine from McCall's, a Montgomery Ward catalog and a personal letter. There was no return address. She opened it without hesitation.

Inside was one of the letters she had written to the orphanages. It had been crumpled up and an attempt had been made to smooth it out. A note was attached.

February 28, 1917

Dear Miss Fairchilds,

I am a novice assigned to St. Anthony's Home here in Washington, D.C. I clean Mother Superior's office and found this letter in the wastebasket. It rolled out at my feet and when I tried to pitch it back in, it rolled at my feet once more. A feeling came over me that I was meant to read it.

Miss Fairchilds, I believe your child is here. I have been careful to match the date of his arrival with the time you expected he would have arrived here. I do not wish to give you false hope, but I would not be comfortable with myself if I did not send this information to you.

If you come to the orphanage, please ask for Sister Mary Claire. We are allowed visitors on Sundays at two in the afternoon. Any Sunday is acceptable.

Please do not write to me as all mail is screened. It is with the danger of being expelled from here that I send this note.

May God bless you,
Sister Mary Claire

Elizabeth burst into tears. They were uncontrolled and made her body shake with her sobbing. She had to get to the back room of the shop before someone came in and found her in such a state.

But, she didn't make it out of the chair before Mary Lee entered. She immediately saw Elizabeth's torment and rushed to her side folding her arms around her. "Miz' Elizabeth, what's wrong?"

Elizabeth could only shake her head and cry.

"Let's get you outta' here before somebody comes in."

The young milliner nodded her head and allowed Mary Lee to lead. By the time they reached the back room, Elizabeth was down to heaving sighs. "I'll...be...all...right...when...I...can... get... my breath."

"I'm gonna' make us some tea," said Mary Lee, in a shaky voice, before tears started rolling down her cheeks.

Elizabeth took a few gulps of air before she could talk calmly for Mary Lee to understand. "I'm sorry. I received a letter in the mail with news I have been hoping for. I wasn't prepared for my reaction. It's happy news, Mary Lee, and although I can't yet tell you what it is, it necessitates my having to take a trip into Washington tomorrow."

Mary Lee wiped away her own tears. "I don't mind tellin' you that you had me mighty worried. Don't never do that agin'."

"I am truly sorry," Elizabeth said and gave her friend a hug. She blew her nose with a flowered hankie from her apron pocket. "Now, let's do get that tea brewing. I can stand a good strong cup."

Mary Lee lit the small kerosene stove while Elizabeth dabbed at her red eyes with a cold washcloth.

"I'll leave in the morning, and I'll be back Sunday night. Once I get things settled you and I are going to have a long talk."

"I surely hope so. Ever since you came back from that weekend at Red Gate Farm you been doin' some strange things. Like yer mind ain't goin' along with yer body."

Elizabeth sighed, "I have been preoccupied. Last week when I inadvertently threw that five dollar bill into the wastebasket instead of the money drawer, I wondered about myself."

Mary Lee gave her a sideways grin. "It ain't been enough to knock them big words outta' yer brain so I guess yer okay. Has it got anythin' to do with Major Caldwell?"

"Not a bit."

"I guess that's good. The tea's ready and I made it strong."

****

The next morning Elizabeth closed the shop. She had imposed enough on Mary Lee and business had been so light she wasn't going to miss much in the way of income by closing the shop for a day. It was Saturday and would give her two days before she had to open on Monday. This was a most important matter that needed immediate attention. If she disappointed a couple of customers by closing the shop for a day, then so be it.

****

She arrived at the Willard around four o'clock in the afternoon.

"Miss Fairchilds, we have Room 216 ready for you. Did you have a good trip in?"

"Very nice, George." she answered. She remembered his name from the last trip.

Apparently, he also remembered her. "Will Major Caldwell be joining you for dinner?" he asked.

Trying to act unruffled, she replied, "Not this evening. Are you expecting Major Caldwell?"

He was clearly embarrassed. "Perhaps I spoke out of turn."

She repeated her question, "Are you expecting Major Caldwell this evening?"

"I believe he made a reservation for six o'clock."

"I would appreciate it if you do not tell him that I will be spending the night here."

"Of course, Miss Fairchilds."

"When is dinner being served?"

"The dining room will open at five o'clock."

She glanced at the clock on the wall. "Good. That will give me enough time to freshen up." An hour ahead of the time Andrew was expected would allow her to miss him and whatever sweet young thing he was escorting. She was irked and deflated.

Elizabeth went up to her room and rested on the bed before she washed her face and hands and patted some powder and rouge on her nose and cheeks. At five minutes before five o'clock she was at the entrance to the dining room and asked the waiter to seat her on the opposite side of the room from Andrew's favorite spot.

At five-thirty, she had finished her supper of ham, sweet potatoes and green beans. She wanted dessert but decided it would take too much time. She needed to be out of the dining room in case Andrew showed up early. How cunning it would be if she could hide and see who accompanied him. Perhaps there was an inconspicuous place in the lobby. The desire was overpowering, but the risk was too great, so she decided to go to her room.

On her way, George, the desk clerk, motioned to her to stop at the desk. "You have a Western Union Telegram."

Her heart almost stopped. No one knew she was there except Mary Lee. She was shaking so; she could hardly open the envelope. Inside was a terse note:

Checked shop…Back lock broken…Robert boarded it up…don't worry… all is fine, Mary Lee.

Elizabeth burst out laughing with relief and marveled at the fact that Mary Lee knew how to send a telegram.

"Is everything all right, Miss Fairchilds?" asked George.

"Sorry if I caused a stir. The message gave me a jolt, but all is fine." Wasn't it like Mary Lee to be so conscientious that she spent money, she couldn't spare, to send a frivolous telegram?

What wasn't fine was that the message had delayed Elizabeth to the point that she heard from the dining room entrance, "Good evening, Major. Your table is ready."

"My party hasn't arrived yet, Harry. I'll wait in the lobby for a few minutes."

Elizabeth didn't turn around. She sidled her way toward the stairs, but before she could reach them a strong arm encircled her waist. "Why Miss Fairchilds," a voice whispered in her ear. "We must hold the record on unexpected meetings."

She was flushed with embarrassment and couldn't bring herself to face him. "How did you know it was me?"

"I can pick you out of a crowd anywhere."

He kept his arm around her waist and the nearness of him gave her goose bumps. When she started to speak, her words came in a flurry, "I apologize. I meant to leave before you arrived, and this is an unplanned trip. I am only here for overnight because I have a meeting tomorrow afternoon, and I should be going to my room before your guest shows up, and I don't want to ruin your evening, and…"

"And, and, and." He turned her to look at him. "Would you like to meet the party that is joining me?"

That brought her to her senses. "Of course not!"

"I think you should," he said as he hooked his arm through hers and pulled her toward the dining room.

Was he angry? She wasn't sure. "Andrew, I don't wish to be humiliated." She tried to hold back but he was insistent.

"Is my party here, Harry?"

"Yes, sir. Seated and waiting for you."

Elizabeth cast her eyes downward and wished she could melt into the floor. Andrew kept a firm grip and headed toward a table, not his usual one, where she lifted her eyes enough to see a couple sitting.

Asa Thomas stood as they approached and acknowledged her. Carolyn reached for her hand. "Elizabeth, how nice to have you join us. Andrew kept this a secret."

"We are all full of secrets," Andrew remarked and winked at Elizabeth.

After dinner and pleasant conversation, the Thomases hurried on home to put Ann Catherine down for the night.

Andrew led Elizabeth to a quiet part of the lobby. They sat on two brocade chairs with a short service table between them. "Now, Elizabeth. I would like an understandable explanation of why you're here without letting me know that you were coming."

"As I attempted to say, I received a letter yesterday that necessitated my being here today.

There wasn't time for me to send you a note. I don't even have your address."

He sat for a moment mulling over what she said, then smiled. "That's very true. I have a letter in the mail with that information, but it must not have reached you yet. Makes me feel better. My first inclination was that you chose not to contact me."

"I would never be that unkind. This will be a short time for me in the city. I will meet with someone tomorrow at two o'clock, and then I will leave on the late train in the evening."

"I don't wish to know who you are meeting with, but I do wish to know if it is an ardent admirer."

He looked so crestfallen Elizabeth had to smile. She reached over and touched his hand. "Andrew, there is no ardent admirer."

He took her hand and pressed it to his lips. "Except me," he confessed. "I have something to tell you. It is in the letter I sent, but I'm glad I have the chance to tell you while we are together. I am being sent to England next week."

"To England? Whatever for?"

"That I can't tell you. It's confidential military business."

"But, you will be coming back?" she asked in alarm.

"Of course, but I don't know when."

"What about Asa? Will he be going with you?"

"Not this time. He has put in one tour over there."

Elizabeth pulled her hand from Andrew's and sat back in her chair. "I'm sorry you're going."

"Not as sorry as I am. Elizabeth, I have to be honest and let you know how I feel. I haven't been able to get you off my mind since that first day we met under the oak tree. I want to stay here, give you a decent courtship, and then I want to marry you."

Her mouth was agape. "That isn't possible, Andrew."

He was persistent. "Why isn't it possible unless you don't care for me and I don't think that's the case. Are you spoken for?"

The truth would come out one day. She leaned toward him and in a quiet voice said, "I have something to tell you. Can we go sit on that settee in the corner?"

"Is it that serious?" he asked in a carefree way.

"It is that serious," she answered, and immediately his manner sobered.

"I'm not sure I want to hear this."

"And, it isn't something I want to tell you, but I must."

He led her from the chair and to the settee with a protective arm around her waist.

They sat side by side.

Elizabeth looked down and twisted the handkerchief she had pulled from her pocketbook.

"I don't know how to say this so I'm just going to say it. I have a child."

He didn't move, and she couldn't raise her eyes to look at him. The silence was unbearable.

Her voice was hardly audible, "Did you hear what I said? I said I have a child."

"I heard," he responded in a dead voice. "Is that what your meeting is about?"

"I think he is in an orphanage here in the city, and I am going to see if the child is my son."

"You gave him up?"

"No. I did not give him up, my parents did."

He reached over and took her hand without speaking, and there they sat, two handsome, dejected bodies lost in their own thoughts.

Finally, Andrew spoke. "It's no wonder you kept it bottled up inside of you. But now you make sense. Why you're in Berryville, why you own the hat shop, why you have been half-hearted in allowing me to get close. The mystery is solved."

There was a sharp edge to her voice. "How do you feel about it? You see, Andrew, I am a tainted woman, and unworthy of a decent man's attention."

"Is that what your mother told you?"

"How did you know?"

He looked at her and took both her hands in his. "Because that sounds like something a mother would say. Elizabeth, it isn't the first time nor is it the last that an attractive, innocent, young lady has been duped. I'm assuming the man was older and well-heeled."

She shrugged her shoulders. "Mother said he was a good catch." Elizabeth continued, "I didn't want to tell anyone until I found my child, but I felt it was only fair for you to know what I'm really like."

This remark angered him and he growled in a low voice. "And what are you really like; a wanton woman of the streets? You are no different from the first day I decided you were for me. I am not without my own transgressions, and I will not judge you!"

Elizabeth was overcome with his words. Right there, in their private little corner, she hugged him with all her might.

Until they had spent the two days together at Red Gate Farm, Elizabeth had looked at Andrew as a convenience. It was unfair, but it was far safer than allowing her feelings to surface. Then the two days spent at Red Gate Farm swept her emotions away. She had come away from that weekend realizing how deeply she cared for him. Now she had bared her soul and he had responded with such empathetic sincerity she knew Andrew Caldwell had bored a place deep into her heart. Had she made another agonizing mistake?

With soft appeal, he asked, "May I go with you tomorrow?"

Elizabeth sat bolt upright. "To the orphanage?"

"To the orphanage," he repeated.

"Andrew, I don't think that wise. This is serious business that may be the downfall of the young woman who wrote to me. She might look on your presence as though I betrayed her confidence."

"I think not. If she is compassionate enough to risk her position, I think she will understand that it would be a difficult task for you to undertake by yourself."

"I don't know, Andrew." She gave it some thought. "I will tell you that I am not looking forward to going alone, and I would feel more confident to have you come with me, but…"

"Then it's settled. We'll both feel better. I'll come by here and we'll take a cab to wherever we need to go."

He stood and offered his hand as Elizabeth rose from the settee.

"Now, it's time for you to get some sleep. I have to get back to the base. We have an eventful day ahead of us." He gave her a gentle kiss and walked her to the foot of the stairs. "Good night, my dear Elizabeth."

"Good night, Andrew."

Chapter 20

Andrew was at the Willard at one-thirty on Sunday afternoon. He waited in the lobby.

Elizabeth wore a conservative navy blue jacket over a long-sleeved, ecru waist and beige skirt. The plain cloche hat matched the skirt. "I'm so nervous I can hardly walk," she said as she met him in the lobby. They went out to the waiting cab.

"Did you get any sleep?' he asked.

"Not a wink."

"Neither did I," he admitted. "Let's be on our way to meet what comes."

"St. Anthony's Home," he told the driver, and they were on their way.

"Are you sure you want to do this?" she asked.

"Would you rather I didn't?"

She patted his hand, "No, I didn't mean it in that way. I need you there because I may not be strong enough." Her voice quavered. "I don't know what I'll do if he isn't my Matthew."

"I think you are a brave young lady to have come through what you have had to endure. Here you've been treated unfairly by the child's father, and your parents, and I haven't seen any sign of cracking."

Elizabeth chuckled. "I guess not."

In a somber tone, she said, "Andrew, if this is my child, I still have to convince my parents to contact the lawyer to rescind their contract. Time is running out. He will be one-year old next month and eligible for adoption. If this child isn't Matthew, I will have to start all over and, by then, it will be too late."

He took her hand. "Let's not think ahead."

"St. Anthony's Home," the driver announced. "Do you want me to wait?"

"Can you return in an hour?"

"Right you are, sir. Back in one hour." He rattled off in the Model-T taxi leaving Elizabeth and Andrew staring at a three-story limestone building with a high fence encircling the yard. They climbed a set of stone steps and rang a bell at the side of a heavy wood door.

A stately nun wearing a flowing black dress opened the door. A stiff white wimple surrounded her face, which was the only part of her body visible aside from her hands. She spoke in a noble voice. "Yes, what is it?"

Elizabeth could hardly speak above a whisper. "We're here to visit with Sister Mary Claire."

"You have eight minutes before visiting hours start. You may come in and wait in the foyer. I will tell Sister that you are here. Are you relatives?"

"No, we are friends."

The woman pointed to two straight chairs. "Please, sit."

177

Elizabeth and Andrew sat and the authoritative nun left. Neither of them spoke. The place was as quiet as a tomb except for the tick-tock of a grandfather's clock. Tick-tock, tick-tock. They both jumped when the clock struck two. Elizabeth covered her mouth to smother an anxious chuckle as Andrew gave her a sideways grin.

A few minutes later a young woman came into the room.

She, too, was dressed head to toe in black. But her dress was slim and straight, unlike the flowing volume of material of the nun who answered the door. The novice's head covering was a simple black material covering her hair and was attached to a white band across her forehead. She stood in front of them with a quiet ease. Andrew had risen from his chair.

"I am Sister Mary Claire," she said.

Elizabeth stood up. "Sister, I am Elizabeth Fairchilds and this is my friend, Major Andrew Caldwell."

The sedate novice acknowledged them both. She whispered to Elizabeth, "Good. You received my note."

"I came as soon as I could."

"Let's walk out into the courtyard."

Andrew and Elizabeth followed her through a hallway where a side door opened into a quiet courtyard planted with small trees hovering above wooden benches. Sister Mary Claire led them to the farthest corner of the yard. The two young women sat together on a bench. Andrew sat apart. This moment belonged to Elizabeth.

With her voice just above a whisper, Sister Mary Claire said, "Miss Fairchilds, I know this baby is your child. I have acquired his birth date, the birth hospital, your name, the lawyer's name and address, and your parents' names and address. Everything matches. I am an assistant to the nun who is in charge of the paperwork for adoptions. Your son's papers came up because there is a couple here in Washington who have put in a request to adopt him."

The information caused her heart to beat faster. "I don't understand why you are doing this if it puts you in jeopardy of being ousted?"

Sister Mary Claire looked directly into Elizabeth's eyes. "Because I have seen other young women in similar circumstances who have never been able to overcome the burden of guilt. And, because I found your letter, I knew that would be your fate. I can only imagine the agony of a parent whose child is taken from her."

The good novice continued, "Mother Superior feels that a child born out of wedlock should be adopted to have the benefit of two parents."

Wedlock! The shameful word grated on her ears. Elizabeth could not stop the color of shame rising in her face. But the novice was a compassionate young woman and the word was not said with malice.

"May I see him?"

179

"We must appear as if I am giving you a tour and you are interested in donating to the home. I will point the child out to you. Before we go, I must instruct you that you are not in any way to show affection toward him. Would your friend like to accompany us?"

"Yes."

"Then I will give him the warning also. You do realize that once you leave today I can be of no further assistance."

"I understand," Elizabeth answered. When they got up from the bench, she felt weak in the knees. Andrew was immediately by her side and took her arm in his. They strolled about with Sister Mary Claire as though they were just interested parties.

Outdoors, they watched older children on a playground. Inside, they toured the older girls' area. Many of those girls served as caretakers for the younger children. Finally, they reached the housing area for the infants. They walked into a large room where cribs and bassinets sat in rows. One part of the room was for play. Sister Mary Claire whispered in Elizabeth's ear, "The child crawling around on the rug is Matthew."

Elizabeth swallowed a lump in her throat and grabbed Andrew's arm. She motioned toward the child. He had blond hair and blue eyes and was engrossed in crawling after a red ball. He didn't seem to notice the strangers enter the room.

Elizabeth watched every move he made. He pushed the ball away and then laughed as he crawled after it. Then he pushed it again and laughed aloud. The ball landed at Elizabeth's feet. She stood immobile. When he reached the ball, he looked up and gave his unknown mother a big smile. She wanted to swoop him up in her arms and run away. She fought back the tears that welled up and squeezed Andrew's arm. She was overcome.

He took the hint. "Thank you so much," he addressed the novice. "I believe we will have to be leaving now."

"Yes. I understand. We can go out this door."

Elizabeth turned back once more to look at her child.

Sister Mary Claire led them back to the foyer where she addressed Elizabeth, "I am relieved you have come. I will earnestly pray that mother and son will be reunited. May God bless you."

The heavy door closed behind them with such finality that Elizabeth started to cry.

Andrew put his arm around her as though to shield her from the world crumbling around her. "You are a strong woman, Elizabeth. Let's walk down the street a bit before the cab comes. You might feel better to get some fresh air."

She held tight to his arm. "Oh, Andrew. He is so beautiful. I don't know what I'll do if I can't get him back."

Andrew's words were meant to soften that possibility. "Have you thought this out, Elizabeth? What if you do get your child back? Will you be able to support him with the income from the hat shop? What about the stories that will be swirling about? And, as your Matthew grows, he may not be accepted. People can be cruel."

Elizabeth did not care for what she heard. "You seem to have given this a lot of thought."

"I'm being realistic."

She had wiped her tears. "Andrew, I wish none of this had happened, but it did. I want my little boy to know his mother. It wasn't my choice to have him taken away from me. If I have to take some hard knocks along the way, then I will have to deal with them. One thing is clear; I will fight for my child and there is no question about that!"

"Then marry me," he said.

She stopped and looked at him. "You are out of your mind."

"No, I am perfectly in my right mind. I love you, Elizabeth. I can adopt Matthew and give him my name."

"Andrew, you don't know what you're saying."

"I know exactly what I'm saying." He got down on one knee in the middle of the sidewalk and took her hand. "Elizabeth Fairchilds, will you marry me?"

"People are staring at us, Andrew."

"Let them stare. I want an answer."

She smiled down on him. "If you want yes or no, then I will have to say no. If you will accept, perhaps, then that is my answer."

He got to his feet. "That's not what I wanted to hear."

"It's the best I can do. Marriage is a very serious consideration."

He held her face in his hands. "I have given it serious consideration. Look directly into my eyes and tell me you don't care for me."

It was all she could do not to melt. "If I recall, you'll be off to England tomorrow and don't know when you'll return. I have to work on getting my child, and I…"

He grabbed her and kissed her. "Let's get married right now."

"It's three o'clock on a Sunday afternoon."

"Yes, but we have a chaplain on the base. We just have to get over there."

Just then, they saw the cab turning the corner on its way to pick them up.

Andrew hailed him down and ushered Elizabeth into the back seat. "Back to the army base," he ordered.

"Andrew," she said, out of the side of her mouth, "I haven't agreed to this."

"Do you want to marry me?"

"I do have deep feelings for you, but I haven't been able to sort them out."

"You can sort them out after we're married."

My God, what was she doing!

"Andrew. I can't possibly just run and get married with gay abandon. Do whatever it is you have to do in England. We'll both have time to think about our decisions."

He was hurt. "I know my decision."

"Besides," she tried to lighten the moment, "you might find an irresistible woman in England who captures your fancy."

His sober countenance did not change. "You are the only one who has captured it permanently."

He tapped the driver on the shoulder. "I've changed my mind. Take us to the Willard Hotel."

They sat in silence as they drove through the streets of Washington. When they reached the hotel, Andrew paid the driver, assisted Elizabeth from the taxi and held her arm as they walked up the steps "Let's have our dinner here," he said. "I can't say as I have much of an appetite, but we do need to eat."

This downcast mood in Andrew was unlike him. Was it due to the visit to the orphanage, the impending trip to England or was it because she had refused his abrupt proposal? What did he expect? She had enough troubles of her own to dwell on. Andrew would have to sort out his own problems.

Harry, the waiter, seated them. Andrew ordered a glass of wine for each of them before giving their dinner orders.

She reached over and touched his hand. "I'm sorry if I've caused you to feel down before you have to go away."

He tightened his hand in hers. "It's not your fault. I have never had the desire to go. Now I find it couldn't have come at a worse time. I should be here to help you through your ordeal. It's going to be a difficult time and you shouldn't have to go through it alone. You've been through enough already."

If she had held any chagrin toward this understanding man sitting here holding her hand, it dissipated with his words.

"What if I don't get him back, Andrew? I've held this hope alive for eleven months. Now that I've seen him, I don't know what I will do if he is adopted. I would always have a gnawing in my soul."

"Don't think like that. Keep the thought ahead of you that he will be coming to you and start to make plans. You look forward to getting Matthew and I'll look forward to getting back from England." He took both her hands in his. "My proposal still stands, and I will expect a definite answer when I return."

Elizabeth smiled at him, "Do you realize what a burden you are putting on me? If I didn't care for you, I would just dismiss the whole idea."

"Ah, but you do care for me." His affable side had returned.

"As I have said before, sometimes you are impossible. I promise I will have my answer when you get back."

He sat in his chair more relaxed.

The waiter placed the wine glasses on the table. "Have an interesting day, sir?" he asked.

"Harry, I have to say that the past two days have been the most surprising days in my life."

The waiter nodded and smiled at Elizabeth. "Your dinners will be right out."

Chapter 21

The train for Bluemont was on time when Elizabeth reached the Alexandria station. She had stayed one more night at the Willard, which meant leaving her shop closed until she arrived in Berryville.

It was a pleasant day, but there were so many thoughts swirling about in her mind she seemed to blot out the outside world. She was so tired. If she had had any sleep in the two days in Washington, she couldn't recall. The mind-muddling events of the weekend were uppermost in her mind.

She thought of Andrew on his way to England, and touched her lips as she recalled the warmth of his kiss and the strength of his embrace when he reluctantly left last evening. They had found a private place in the lobby of the Willard for their farewell. Was it the hand of Providence that her heart should be torn into pieces?

Andrew's last words had been more like an order. "Go to your parents as soon as you can and get started on getting Matthew back."

She hated to have to face her parents. Formidable as the burden was she knew he was right.

Andrew said he would write as soon as he was settled. Now, she would have to be content to look forward to that time. Elizabeth settled into the train car trying to think of anything that would take her mind off her troubles.

A young mother came toward her carrying a baby wrapped in a light knitted shawl.

"May I sit next to you?" she asked.

"Please do."

Elizabeth helped the young woman with a tote bag she was juggling along with a large pocketbook. The young mother gingerly slid into the seat. "Sometimes Jenny gets fussy if we're on the train too long, I'm trying not to wake her."

"How old is she?" asked Elizabeth.

"Just turned six months. Too old to depend on her staying asleep and not old enough to keep herself occupied. Do you have children?"

"No," answered Elizabeth, which was on the shade of truth.

The woman eased the shawl from around the child's face and arms. "Well, they are a lot of work, but I wouldn't trade this one for anything. She has captured her father's heart as well as mine." She patted the baby and held her close. "I'm going all the way to Leesburg to visit my parents. They aren't travelers so I feel it's my duty to bring Jenny out every few weeks. Otherwise they get out of sorts. I don't think they realize what a chore it is for me to make all the arrangements."

"Parents can be unfeeling at times," agreed Elizabeth. How well she knew. "It is fortunate they want to be close to your baby and welcome you both."

As though this were a revelation, the young mother looked directly at Elizabeth. "I hadn't thought of it in that way. Thank you. I shall keep that uppermost in my mind when I'm feeling vexed at having to make all the preparations."

Elizabeth smiled and brought a book out of her travel bag. The talk of parents was beginning to stir unpleasant feelings and she had had enough of them. What was the likelihood of her parents even wanting to see either she or Matthew if she were successful in getting him back? Her father had mellowed, but what of her mother? An idea came out of the blue. She had to convince her father to rescind the agreement her parents had with the lawyer. Then it would be up to him to persuade her mother. Yes, that would be the best approach. Satisfied she had come to a firm decision, Elizabeth felt some of the tension leave her body.

The young mother was satisfied with cradling and cuddling her child in silent admiration. As the train slowed when it neared the Leesburg station, the baby awoke with a soft whimper, which quickly escalated into a startled cry. The mother cooed and rocked and pulled a rattle from her bag. The little one quieted with the soothing sound of her mother's voice and was distracted by the sound of the rattle, which she grasped in a tight fist.

Elizabeth looked up from her book. "She is a pretty baby," she told the proud mother.

"Thank you. I believe all parents think their child is beautiful so when it comes from someone else it holds meaning."

Elizabeth surrendered to a wave of self-pity. She has already missed this time with her child and she could never get it back. How she wanted to feel his little hand in hers, to lift him up and hold him tight knowing he was of her flesh and blood and would be hers forever. No matter what she had lost, there was promise ahead.

When the train pulled into the Leesburg station, baby Jenny's patience had reached its limit. "She's hungry," the mother apologized. "I'm glad we made it to here before she gets to the point of no return. I'm still nursing her so I'll have to find a private spot inside the station."

"Can I be of any help? This is a fifteen minute stop," said Elizabeth.

"If you could help with my bag or my purse, I would most certainly appreciate it."

By this time, the baby had set up a ruckus much to the embarrassment of the mother.

"Let's go," said Elizabeth. "You concentrate on Jenny. I'll carry both bags and be right behind you."

They hurried off the train car with annoyed passengers staring at them as they left.

"Train'll be pullin' out in about ten minutes," advised the conductor.

"Don't leave without me," ordered Elizabeth.

Once inside the station they found a secluded spot behind a wooden partition.

Elizabeth held the howling baby while the harried mother prepared to nurse the upset infant. In between sucking sounds and sobs, the baby settled into the comforts of her mother's milk.

The young mother was grateful. "Thank you so much. I don't even know your name."

"It isn't important," said Elizabeth. "Will you be all right now?"

"Yes. If you happen to see an older couple looking worried, that will most likely be my parents. Their last name is Cooper."

"If I run into them, I'll tell them where you are."

"Thank you again. I am so sorry for the trouble we caused you."

"I'm glad I could be of help," answered Elizabeth. She patted the baby in the mother's arms and left to return to the train. Before boarding, she did indeed see a couple looking anxious. "Mr. and Mrs. Cooper?"

They looked at her and nodded.

"Your daughter and grandchild are behind the second partition to the left."

Elizabeth continued on, while the two looked at each other with a bewildered look before they entered the station.

Elizabeth settled into her former seat and felt an inner glow of satisfaction as the train headed for Bluemont.

On arrival in Berryville, Herbert Marks pulled the long twelve-passenger car to the side of Main Street in front of the hotel, which Elizabeth entered before going to her apartment. She went straight to the phone and dialed her parents' number. A familiar voice answered, "Fairchilds' residence."

"Opal, this is Elizabeth. Is my father home?"

"Yes, child. He's in his study. Are you all right?"

"Yes, I'm fine. I must talk to my father."

In seconds, her father was on the other end of the line. "Elizabeth, what's the matter?"

"Father, I'm going to talk fast. I have an urgent matter that needs to be attended to right away. Look for a letter in the mail within the next few days. I am asking a favor of you and mother."

"Is everything all right, Elizabeth?"

"Yes, all is fine, but I can't talk about this over the phone. It is in regards to your agreement with the lawyer."

"I'm not sure I understand."

"You have got to let me know if you don't receive the letter by Friday. Call me here at the hotel."

"I have the number. You're sure you're all right?"

"I'm fine. You will understand, once you receive my letter, why this is imperative. Tell mother I send my regards. I love you, Father. Goodbye."

Elizabeth hung up the phone before he could respond. Then she hurried over to her apartment, where she put water over for tea and pulled out stationery to pen the letter; it would have to go out in the morning post.

191

March 20, 1917

Dear Father,

Please forgive my hurried phone call on Monday evening. I hope it didn't alarm you. I must be careful of what I say over the phone because one never can be sure who might be listening.

I have found Matthew. He is in St. Anthony's Home (orphanage) in Washington. It is certainly not a place to raise a child in my opinion. He is a beautiful little one. I watched him crawl and play with a ball. According to the novice, Sister Mary Claire, who took us through the place, he can pull himself up to stand but he is not yet walking.

Are you and mother satisfied with not knowing your grandson?

My urgent request is that you convince mother that you have to rescind your contract with the lawyer. Time is running out. Next month he will be one-year old and the adoption can go forward. From my understanding, there is an influential couple in Washington, who has the means, and want to adopt him. We cannot let that happen. He belongs with his family!

Father, I am begging you. Mother and I are not on the best terms so I must place this burden upon your shoulders. I would so like to be a family once again.

I believe we must settle this within the next
two weeks or I feel I will lose my precious
son forever.

> *Your loving and*
> *pleading daughter,*
> *Elizabeth*

She would have sealed it with her tears if she thought it would do any good. Donning her shawl and bonnet, she rushed over to the post office and placed it in the night slot so that it would go out first thing in the morning.

Back at her apartment, she found she had been so distracted about getting the letter written she had forgotten to light the fire under the teakettle. Confident and relieved she had done what she could to get the information to her father, she felt the gnawing pang of hunger. She set about fixing fried potatoes and eggs while she waited to relish her cup of tea. The week would be one of waiting and hoping for her father's agreement.

The next morning Mary Lee was at the shop early. "I'm glad you got back all right, Miz' Elizabeth. You 'bout scared me to death runnin' off that fast. An' then when you wasn't here yesterday to open the shop, I went and did it. Ol' Miz' Talley came nosin' around. I told her you had an important meetin'. She wanted to know what about. I wanted to tell her it was none of her business, but I just smiled and said I wasn't sure. An', that wasn't a fib 'cause I didn't know."

"Thank you for tending the shop. Let's sit. You may not believe what I am about to tell you."

Mary Lee looked skeptical but she dutifully took a seat in the back room of the shop where Elizabeth had been busy straightening out the storage area.

"Do you remember when I went out to Red Gate Farm with Andrew Caldwell and determined not to let him affect me?"

"How could I forgit that?"

"Well, I met him while I was in Washington. It was purely unexpected. He has gone to England for some secret military thing, so we had dinner together on Saturday evening with the Thomases."

"Miz' Carolyn?"

"Yes. Then we spent most of Sunday together. I had an important meeting and Andrew went with me. Mary Lee, I think I am in love with him."

"You and half the girls in this county."

"I've found him to be a man with deep feelings and he cares for me. He asked me to marry him."

"Oh, no, Miz' Elizabeth. What did you say?"

"I told him I would not be able to give him an answer until he returned."

"But, Miz' Elizabeth, he's known as a ladies' man. I hear that kind can break a girl's heart. I'd feel right bad if that happened to you."

"Mary Lee, how long did you know Robert before you said, yes?"

Mary Lee thought about it. "Wal', you got a point there. But, I was married to a no account before and I knew what to look for."

"And, I'm not pristine," answered Elizabeth.

"Whatever that means," mumbled Mary Lee.

The tinkling of the bell, signaling a customer, interrupted their conversation.

"We'll discuss this later," said Elizabeth.

Chapter 22

Each day was torture until the letter from Francis Fairchilds arrived. The minute Lloyd Pierce left the shop, Elizabeth ran to the back room. With shaking hands, she ripped open the envelope and unfolded the missive.

March 27, 1917

Dear Elizabeth,

I'm sure you have been anxious to hear some word from me. I apologize for not sending a note earlier to let you know where we are in the process regarding Matthew.

It took much persuasion on my part to get your mother to even listen to my proposal. I told her about your urgent telephone call, but it did not sway her from the opinion that you are better off not being burdened with a child.

I understand her view. But, I must tell you that I went to St. Anthony's Home by myself. I asked for Sister Mary Claire as you had written. She was most helpful. Even though she pointed the little fellow out to me, it wasn't necessary. He reminded me of you when you were a baby. He has the same coloring and what appears to be a most delightful personality. Although he seems to

196

be well cared for, that is no place for him or any of the others for that matter. I thought the nuns to be overly strict with the older children. To be honest, I could hardly wait to leave.

When I told your mother what I had done, she blew like the whistle on a teakettle. It mattered not because once she calmed down we were able to have a sensible conversation.

This time I have set down the law and she will be going with me to see Jacob Cunningham to undo what we have done. My God! What were we thinking?

I will telephone as soon as we have seen the lawyer and let you know the outcome. I do not remember all he advised when we signed to have the baby put up for adoption. Those days are a haze.

Although our time is running short, try to rest easy with the thought that we are determined to do all we can.

> *We both send*
> *our best regards,*
> *Your loving father*

****

The millinery shop was busy with the Easter season approaching. Elizabeth was tired of the heavy materials of the cold winter months and was almost happy to be working with the lighter straws and bright pastels, although, hat making was still not to her liking. She wished Catherine Burke would once again find some outdated inventory and send it on. In the fashion world, Berryville would always be behind the times to the young milliner's way of thinking.

This morning she was vexed. Mary Lee was spending less time in the shop now she and Robert were engaged. It was Mary Lee who held the creative edge. Elizabeth knew what looked good but the actual hands on labor of getting it onto the hat was beyond her capabilities.

It had been over two weeks since Andrew had left for England. She had expected some word from him, but there had been none.

And, where were her parents in the process of dealing with the lawyer, Jacob Cunningham? She had been tempted to call them but she knew that would only serve to aggravate the situation. Her father said he would notify her as soon as they had news and he was one to keep his word. Patience was not one of Elizabeth's strong qualities.

When Mary Lee arrived around ten o'clock that morning, Elizabeth was at the peak of aggravation.

"It's about time you got here. I am up to my ears in trying to get ready for spring and you have been too busy to help me out!"

Mary Lee was speechless. She looked at her friend with wide eyes before sporting a grin. "Why, Miz' Elizabeth, I 'spect somethin' is botherin' you."

"I'm sorry. I have so many things on my mind, I could just scream!"

Mary Lee walked to the counter and picked up a hat. "Maybe you should try runnin' aroun' yer backyard hollerin' loud as you can."

Elizabeth stood with hands on hips. "Now what good would that do?"

"Let you run off some steam." Mary Lee pulled out a chair and began to work on the hat she was holding before she added, "Course, runnin' an' hollerin' might make you look kind of crazy."

That brought Elizabeth to a more acceptable mood. "All right. I think I'm down to a simmer."

"Good," said her friend as she picked up some sea-blue ribbon to trim the hatband. "If you go out and slam the teakettle on the stove, you can simmer up a cup of tea."

"I'll do that. We can both use a cup. Do you want me to read your tealeaves?"

"Not unless yer over yer snit. I'm afraid of what you'd see."

Elizabeth marched to the back room and Mary Lee heard the metal of the teakettle hit the burner on the kerosene stove. A satisfied smile crept to the corners of her mouth.

When Elizabeth returned, Mary Lee held up the hat. She had fashioned a large rosette bow with white and blue ribbon to match the hatband.

"What do you think? Should I put some of this chiffon behind it to make it stand out?" She wove the white chiffon in such a manner that it almost made the flower come alive.

199

"Oh, what a perfect touch. You finish the trim and I'll pour the tea."

"Soon as I git this knotty mess together, I'll be ready for some. What made you so upset this mornin'? Somethin' I should know?" She cut the thread with her teeth.

"Lots of different things all came to a head. There are times when I don't think I can handle it."

Elizabeth took a seat opposite while Mary Lee threaded another needle.

"I 'spect it either has somethin' to do with Major Caldwell or stayin' cooped up in this place all the time."

"I've been going to Sunday services."

"But, you don't come when Robert and I invite you anymore."

"I don't want to be in the way."

"If you was, we wouldn't keep askin'."

"I don't want you to feel sorry for me."

Mary Lee put the finished hat on the counter. "We don't need to. You do enough of that fer all of us. I'm ready fer the tea an' whatever else you want to throw my way. Somethin's been troublin' you ever since you came here."

Elizabeth poured the refreshment. Did she dare tell her friend about Matthew? She decided to wait.

"You are right about Andrew. I haven't heard a word since he left and he promised to write when he got settled in England."

"Maybe he ain't settled yet."

Elizabeth sipped her tea. "I would think he would be after this period of time."

"Maybe it takes a long time for letters to get across the ocean. However they do it."

"You are probably right, it hasn't been enough time for his correspondence to reach me."

Mary Lee stirred her tea. "Miz' Elizabeth, I know you were right upset about me not bein' here as much. I'll try to be better about it."

"I don't begrudge you your time with Robert. I'm happy for you. It's just that I have to keep this shop going and you are so much help with the hats and knowing which customers like what. I can give you a lady's name and you know instantly what suits her."

"You know it too. You just ain't interested in that part of yer business. Now, the jewelry and accessories are somethin' yer good at. Seems every woman that walks in here goes out with somethin' even if it ain't --- isn't---a hat."

Elizabeth smiled as she heard Mary Lee correcting herself.

"Miz' Catherine used to get on me all the time for usin' ain't. But, I been usin' it all my life so it ain't easy to break an old habit. I wish I knew some of the big words you and Miz' Catherine use."

"We could work together on that. I can give you some words and you can look them up in my dictionary. I have one upstairs you can borrow."

Mary Lee shook her head. "Too much work. Besides, Robert and all his family talk like me and they'd think I was tryin' to git uppity."

Elizabeth smiled. Mary Lee Thompson was so comfortable in her life that she felt a twinge of jealousy. "How do you do it?"

Mary Lee looked over her teacup. "Do what?"

"How do you get to be so easy and comfortable with life?"

"If you'd grown up like I did and lived with Zack Thompson, you'd learn not to 'spect too much out of life."

Elizabeth looked over and smiled at her friend. "Are you ready for me to read your leaves? I'm dying to see signs of what your wedding is going to be like. That's only nine weeks away."

"Don't remind me. That's been worryin' me."

"Why don't we make the plans together?" Elizabeth suggested.

A look of relief crossed Mary Lee's face. "Would you help me? I haven't asked 'cause you been so caught up in what's been botherin' you, I didn't want to ask. You know more about what's proper than I do. Robert is the one who wants this to be special. Me, I'd just like to run to a Justice of the Peace, say the words, and sign a paper."

Elizabeth's spirits had lifted. "Oh, that would take all the joy out of it. Robert is right to make this a special time. You have wiped the clouds from my day, dear friend. We shall begin planning to make this a most celebratory affair."

Mary Lee cocked her head. "An' that's good?"

"That's outstanding!"

Chapter 23

On April 6th, Mary Lee and Elizabeth were busy at the work counter in the hat shop when Lavinia Talley burst through the door gasping for air. Elizabeth was out of her chair in a flash.

"Mrs. Talley, what's wrong?"

Lavinia fanned her ample bosom. "I must c…c…catch my b…b…breath."

"Is it Mr. Talley?" Elizabeth asked in alarm.

Lavinia shook the question away with a wave of her hand. She made one last gasp before she spoke.

"Jeremy has just received news that President Wilson has severed diplomatic relations with Germany and has declared our country at war!"

Mary Lee jumped up from her chair knocking hats off the counter in her haste.

"Are you sure Mrs. Talley? There can be no mistake?" asked Elizabeth.

Lavinia set her jaw firm. "I am not one to carry tales. Jeremy got word by telegram from a source in Washington. Now, I must hustle on up the street to let others know."

When she left, the two young ladies stood looking at one another.

"What do you think this means, Miz' Elizabeth?"

"Before Andrew left he said he was afraid we might be dragged into this war. Perhaps that is why I haven't heard from him."

Mary Lee started wringing her hands. "Do you 'spose Robert might have to go in the army? Maybe we won't be gettin' married after all."

"Let's not jump to conclusions. We don't know the whole story, and I'm not going to trust Mrs. Talley to give us the information." Those reassuring words were meant only for Mary Lee. Elizabeth's thoughts had immediately gone to Andrew and the possibility that he might not return from England.

"Let's get back to work. We have to get a good spring inventory sold before people panic and stop spending money."

They took their places at the work counter in silence. Each young woman made an effort to keep her shaking hands still and tried not to think of the ramifications of a declaration of war.

Later that morning Lloyd Pierce brought the mail by. He was not his usual affable self. "I guess Miz' Talley's been here already."

"About an hour ago," Elizabeth answered.

"Yeah, she's flittin' all over town with the news. Before she's done she'll probably say that every able-bodied man in the county has been signed up. The woman can spin a story faster than a spider can spin a web."

He winked and smiled at Elizabeth before he hoisted his bag on his shoulder. "You might be lookin' for this mail, Miz' Elizabeth. Here it is all the way from England with Major Andrew Caldwell's name on it. See you next time." Off he went delivering the cherished mail.

Elizabeth snatched the letter off the counter.

Mary Lee had recovered from her initial reaction to Lavinia's news and was hard at work. "It's what you been waitin' for. I said maybe it would be a spell before he was settled. Do you think he knows about this war business?"

"It wouldn't be in this letter," Elizabeth answered as she opened the envelope with the silver letter opener. "Not unless it has something to do with the reason he was sent over there in the first place." She unfolded the letter and read silently while Mary Lee busied herself with a hat.

March 23, 1917

My dearest Elizabeth,

Finally, I have a few minutes to write. This has been a tiresome journey thus far. The sea was choppy all the way and left me so ill that I could eat but little. I have lost ten pounds.

When we arrived in London, I was to stay in the city with one of the officers of the British navy. Something went awry and I had no sooner reached his place, when I received word that I would be quartered in

206

another officer's home outside the city. By that time I was so tired and worn out that I never budged from the house all the next day.

I find my room quite comfortable. The countryside is a lush green with spring flowers already in bloom. My host, Major Nelson, is about my age and has three children. The youngest is a couple of months older than your Matthew. Be prepared for when your son comes to live with you. I expect he will show a willingness to explore whatever comes in his path. At least that is what I have observed from the little one here.

On the subject of Matthew, how have you fared regarding your parents, the lawyer, and the Catholics? How I wish I could be there to help you through this process. Do try to patch up the rift with your parents. I assume they would like nothing better than to have their lovely daughter back in their fold.

I can only say that I find myself caring more for you as each minute goes by. My thoughts wander when I am idle, and I picture what it will be like when I return home. You have promised me an answer to my proposal and I pray with all my heart it will be in my favor. We have had so little time together, but I can recall each precious moment.

I will work diligently on this task I have been given so that I can return as soon as this assignment is completed. Bear in mind there are always unforeseen circumstances that could get in the way.

I will be searching the mail for your erstwhile reply. Until then, know that you are in my thoughts each waking moment, my dear Elizabeth.

All my love,
Andrew

She carefully folded the letter and placed it in her apron pocket.

She gave a heavy sigh before she spoke, "He gives no hint that he knows anything about us being dragged into a war. He is staying in the home of a Major Nelson and says that it is quite comfortable."

"Does he say when he will come back?" asked Mary Lee.

Elizabeth took her seat. "He gives no definite time but hopes to wind up his assignment and return as soon as that is done, barring any unforeseen circumstances. I guess the declaration of war would fit into that category."

Mary Lee shrugged her shoulders and sat back in her chair. "I swear, Miz' Elizabeth, everythin' in my life has changed so much. First Miz' Catherine got married and left, then you come along, then I met Robert and we're suppose' to be gettin' married, and then you met Major Caldwell and most likely will get married, an' now we got the war to worry about. I cain't think of any more that would surprise me."

"Life is full of surprises, Mary Lee, some good and some bad. We just have to learn to take them as they come or we would all be ready for the booby hatch."

Mary Lee laughed. "I 'spect yer right. Miz' Elizabeth, you do make me smile."

****

That evening Elizabeth lay awake for hours wishing she could take the advice she'd given her friend. Too many troublesome thoughts swirled through her head. Time was running short and she hadn't heard a word from her father since last week. She tried to push Andrew out of her mind, but with this news about the war, she could only hope he would return from England before American troops would be sent to Europe. Even if he finished his work earlier, he wouldn't be back until the end of April. The thought brought a lump to her throat.

Elizabeth got out of bed and went to the kitchen for a drink of water. She took two aspirins hoping the medicine would help her get to sleep. She looked in the mirror on the dressing table before she got back into bed and was appalled at the dark circles under her eyes.

Why hadn't she heard any news from her father? Instead of crawling into bed she packed her valise with necessities because the first train in the morning would find her on the way to Washington.

****

Opal answered Elizabeth's knock when she arrived at her parents' home in Alexandria. A look of joy lit up her face. "Why Miz' Elizabeth! Come in, child."

"Are my parents at home?"

"They're in the dining room just sitting down for lunch."

Her father came into the foyer. "Elizabeth, what a surprise! I thought I recognized your voice."

"I was going to call, Father, but I didn't have time."

He came forward and kissed her on the cheek. "Come in and have lunch with us, while you tell us what brings this unexpected pleasure."

How could he be so calm? Elizabeth was tied up in knots but she kept her composure.

"Hello, Elizabeth," said her mother without turning to face her. "Yes, come in and have lunch. Opal, we will need a place set for Miss Elizabeth."

"Hello, Mother. I apologize for getting here at lunchtime." She knew her mother didn't like to have unexpected guests.

Francis Fairchilds seated Elizabeth to face her mother.

"I'm sure you know why I am here. I want to know what progress has been made regarding Matthew."

Opal set a plate before her and poured tea.

"I told you I would call when we had something firm. We hope to hear from Jacob today."

"Time is growing short, Father. I have to know and, if there is something I can do, I am here to do it."

Opal brought potato soup and ladled it into their bowls, while her father passed a basket of sliced bread.

"This isn't the time to discuss it," her mother admonished.

"Opal knows what's going on," Elizabeth shot back.

"Let's be civil," her father cautioned.

Their attention reverted to the soup in front of them, and the colored maid discretely left the room.

Her father began, "Elizabeth, we talked with the lawyer, yesterday. He has presented our papers to the people who run the orphanage saying we have changed our minds about having Matthew adopted and wish to have him come back into our family."

Potato soup fell off her spoon. "What did they say?"

"It's become a bit complicated. The Mother Superior, who is head of the home, is against it. Her opinion is, according to Jacob, that we are too old, and, if the mother is wanting the child, she wouldn't be suitable."

"Not suitable? She doesn't even know me!"

Gertrude Fairchilds sat across from her daughter quietly sipping tea. "I assume she is

211

considering the circumstances under which Matthew was born."

Francis Fairchilds cleared his throat. "That's enough, Mother. We have to discuss this. Anyway, we also talked to the priest who apparently handles this kind of thing and he is in favor of rescinding the adoption order, but, because there is such a difference of opinion, he is sending the matter to the bishop to decide. It seems the couple who want to adopt Matthew are of the Catholic faith and are influential in the Washington circles."

"So what does this mean?" asked Elizabeth.

"It means nothing will be settled until the bishop rules on the information he has been given. Matthew will stay where he is until that time."

Tension eased out of her body. "That is some consolation. At least we have more time. Do you think it would help if I went to see Mr. Cunningham?"

Her father gave her a benevolent smile. "I believe we will have to let the matter rest until we hear further."

"Perhaps I will go to see the bishop."

'Elizabeth," came her father's gentle voice. "I believe it would be almost impossible for that to take place. He is a busy and powerful man. This adoptive couple must wield some authority."

"But, he is a man, Father, and my child is at stake."

"Let's give it a bit more time. The lawyer is working for us and the priest is on our side. It wouldn't do to upset the apple cart."

Elizabeth slumped. "I suppose you are right, but I am anxious to get on with it."

"As we all are," her father replied. "Would you care for another piece of bread?"

"No thank you, I haven't finished this one. Mother have you seen Matthew?"

Gertrude gave a hard glance at her husband. "Your father insisted that he go alone."

"Isn't Matthew beautiful, Father?"

"He is a fine looking boy."

Gertrude Fairchilds gave a deep sigh. "You must realize this has been a very difficult time for us. We had such hopes and dreams for you and they were all washed away. When we had just about resolved we had done the right thing, all this heartache surfaced again. Elizabeth, if the child is unable to come back to us, we may carry that guilt for the rest of our lives."

She looked at her parents. "You don't know how many times I have been sorry for the worry and shame I have brought to both of you. I want your forgiveness so we can start anew. Matthew is ours. We will just have to make, whoever the bishop is, see it that way."

For the first time Elizabeth could remember Gertrude Fairchilds had tears in her eyes. Elizabeth rushed from her chair and put her arms around her mother's neck and pressed cheek to cheek.

She held her daughter's hands. "I just couldn't bear to see your life fade away."

"Do you think we can start again?"

"You have been forgiven, Elizabeth, many months ago, but I just couldn't show it."

Elizabeth kissed her mother and went to her father. "I had intended to stay the night, but, if I hurry, I can catch the last train back to Bluemont. I closed the shop and I can ill afford it with spring upon us. Do you think you could give me a lift to the Alexandria station?"

He patted her hand, "Of course. Mother, would you care to ride along with us?"

Gertrude Fairchilds finished dabbing her eyes and gave a wan smile. "If you can wait for me to find my shawl."

Opal held the front door as the three prepared to leave. On her way out, Elizabeth threw her a kiss. In return, Opal spread a big grin and gave an affirmative nod of her head.

****

Back at the Bluemont station, Elizabeth stood on the porch outside while Herbert Marks loaded baggage into the twelve-passenger car. The air smelled of spring and brought a sense of rebirth to Elizabeth's improved mood. As soon as she returned to her apartment, she would pen a letter to Andrew. She thought of him almost as much as he professed to be thinking of her.

When the long car was ready, Elizabeth took a seat.

"Miz' Elizabeth you sure do a lot of travelin' to and from the city," remarked Herbert.

Elizabeth just smiled.

The car made its way down the mountain as dusk was setting in. As they motored up the main street of the town of Berryville, Herbert pulled the car to the side of the street. She carried her satchel as she departed the vehicle. Herbert helped her out of the car advising her to watch her step. "Goin' back to the city again?" he asked.

She was not about to give herself away. "One never knows. Thank you for the safe trip back."

He tipped his cap and watched as she crossed the street, mounted the four steps to her stoop and unlocked the door before she turned to give him a wave. Upstairs, Elizabeth put the kettle over for tea before selecting stationery to write to Andrew. She could hardly wait to put words on paper.

April 12, 1917

My dear Andrew,

I received your most welcome letter, and I am happy all is going well for you after a very bad start. It makes my stomach queasy just to think about a ship bobbing up and down. I think I shall never be brave enough to go across the sea.

I have just returned from Washington with good news. It is not exactly what I had hoped for, but it has given me some relief to know that all is not lost concerning Matthew. His fate is in the hands of the Catholic bishop. Meanwhile, he will remain at St. Anthony's Home until his Lordship, or whatever one calls a Catholic bishop, makes a decision. Understandably, I am concerned about the outcome. Enough of this downhearted talk!

On the bright side, I have made up with my parents, which you had been so wise to advise. Father and I had been of the same mind, but Mother was more difficult to convince. Mother says if the adoption papers cannot be rescinded, she isn't sure she can stand the heartache it will cause. I am not sure I could either, but I am of a set mind to feel optimistic. Pessimism never wins.

Just as you are eager to come back home, I am equally as eager to have you here. This Declaration of War has all of us in a state of unrest. I pray it will not come to the point of having to send our loyal military boys over to Europe.

When I waved goodbye to you on our last meeting, I didn't realize how much I would miss you. I believe Matthew, not born under the best of circumstances, has been the Almighty's way of bringing us together.

I send you my love.

> *Affectionately,*
> *Elizabeth*

Chapter 24

People were beginning to worry about conserving money now the country was at war. This was not good news for Elizabeth. Nevertheless, spring inventory in the hat shop sold as well as she had hoped. By the first of May she was in a dilemma whether to shore up the dwindling hat supply or increase the price of those she had on hand. The trend in the millinery business was less adorned hats with smaller brims. That meant adjusting to the acceptable guidelines.

It was said that even President Wilson was doing his part for the war effort by running a herd of sheep on the White House lawn. Their wool was to be donated to the Red Cross.

It was also reported that the first troops would be sent to Europe in June.

Where was Andrew involved in this mess? Elizabeth had received only one more letter with little information except that he missed her. He was upset about the war business but had given no indication that he was privy to any more information.

After opening for the day, Elizabeth was sweeping the floor of the shop when the usually abrasive Ruth Caldwell entered the front door. This was a surprise, as Elizabeth had not seen her since the weekend she spent at Red Gate Farm.

Tucking the broom into a corner, the young milliner smoothed her apron before she went to greet Ruth.

"Good morning, Miss Caldwell."

"You might as well call me Ruth. Mother has sent me in to invite you out to Red Gate Farm for this weekend."

Elizabeth managed to appear unruffled. "Is there a special reason?"

"Mother gets these whims. I suppose it might have to do with Andrew. I understand the two of you have been keeping company. It is difficult for me to keep up with Andrew's infatuations."

Her words were like a slap in the face. Ruth's arrogant attitude did not set well with Elizabeth. "You may tell Mrs. Caldwell that I appreciate the invitation, but I have plans for this weekend. As far as Andrew's and my relationship, that is between the two of us."

Ruth closed her gaping jaw. "Do you mean to tell me that you are turning down Mother's request?"

"I do. Please extend my apologies. This must have been a distasteful task for you, Miss Caldwell, but, if you have no other reason to be here, I beg your pardon as I have work to do."

Ruth Caldwell was not used to being dismissed. Her face flushed scarlet to the roots of her auburn hair before she turned on her heel and went out the door nearly knocking Mary Lee off the stoop.

"Land sakes, Miz' Elizabeth, what set her off?" asked the startled Mary Lee as she closed the door behind her.

Elizabeth watched out a corner of the window as the driver held the door for Ruth to get into the fashionable touring car. She slammed her pocketbook onto the rear seat as the car pulled away.

Elizabeth turned back from the window. "I'm afraid I did. She came, at her mother's request, to ask me to come out to Red Gate Farm this weekend. Why, I don't know! Nor do I care! I don't want to disappoint Andrew's mother, but I have more important things on my mind."

"She's sure got you riled up and I ain't sayin' a word."

"Perhaps I was too short with her but I was not about to acquiesce to her haughty way."

Mary Lee gave a wry smile, "There you go throwin' them big words aroun' agin'. Jus' think, she might turn out to be yer sister-in-law. Really got your dander up, didn't she?"

"The woman is irritating. I think I'll clean that mirror."

She immediately began rubbing the mirror with gusto. "What do you think causes brothers and sisters to be disagreeable with one another? I always yearned for a brother or sister."

Mary Lee replied, "Jealousy, maybe. I don' know. I got two brothers. The older one moved on when he turned seventeen and we never heard from him agin'. My other brother has a job over at Audley Farm. I run into him every once't in a while, but we don't keep company no more 'cause he's so busy. But, there ain't nothin' I wouldn't do for him if I had to."

"What were your parents like?"

"Wal', my daddy died when I was nine, not that we saw much of him 'cause he went to work 'afore we got up and went right to bed after supper. Then my gramma died when I was ten. Then my momma ran off with some man passin' through town. My brother and I got farmed out to my momma's sister, and she didn't want us, but we were good extra help."

Elizabeth stopped cleaning and turned to look at her friend. "Mary Lee, that's terrible. Why didn't you tell me this before?"

"I can't say as I'm proud of it so it's not likely somethin' I'm goin' to blab around. Especially with the kind of life you had."

Elizabeth put her cleaning supplies in a basket and came to sit at the work counter. "I guess you're right. I don't ever think I fully appreciated what my parents did for me."

"Maybe Andrew and his brother and sister don't get along, Miz' Elizabeth, 'cause they done had it too easy. If you don't have hardships, you don't know how good you got it."

"Are you going to invite your brother to the wedding?"

Mary Lee shot her a look of disbelief. "Course I am. And, speakin' of my weddin', its comin' up next month. Don't seem like we've spent much time on it. I'm beginnin' to get antsy."

"I haven't been idle. I have a list made that we can go over together and you change anything you like. You've got Irene Butler making your dress and that's most important."

"That's true, an', I've got my hat almost put together." Mary Lee got out of her chair and started toward the back room. "I'm goin' to put the kettle over. I could use a cup of tea. How about you?"

"I can always use a cup of tea," answered Elizabeth.

When Mary Lee returned with the tea tray, Elizabeth had her wedding list on the work counter. "I haven't read your tealeaves in a while. Do you want me to read them today?"

"I sure wish you would read yer own one of these days. Might be all the Caldwells are jumbled up in there."

And, my beautiful Matthew, Elizabeth thought, but she wouldn't risk reading her own leaves. Mary Lee still did not know about her sweet little one stuck away in that orphanage. Elizabeth ached to tell her although the time was still not right, so she kept her silence as she sipped her tea. "Jumbled is a good word to describe my life. I did get something straightened out on this last quick trip into Washington. I made up with my parents."

Mary Lee paused. "You don't never talk much 'bout yer parents. I knew somethin' wasn't right when they came by fer Thanksgivin'. Not doin' what they wanted you to do?"

Elizabeth brushed her blond curls away from her face. "That's part of it."

"I 'spect there's a lot more I don't need to know."

"Not just yet, but, as I've told you. One of these days we're going to have a long talk." Elizabeth sat her teacup on the china saucer. "What do you think of Andrew? Has Robert ever said anything about tales he's heard? I know men like to gossip as well as women do."

Mary Lee gave her a kindly smile. "That's where you first met, Major Caldwell, wasn't it, that day we had our picnic at the Mitchell's place?"

Elizabeth nodded in agreement. "And, I wasn't even nice to him. That seems so long ago. I guess change happens when we least expect it. Never would I have dreamed I would be in a quandary over a proposal of marriage from him."

With a self-conscious lift of her eyelids, Mary Lee confessed, "Robert and me talked about it 'cause I was mighty upset you could get hurt. I don't know what's caused it, but I think you've had enough bad happen already."

Elizabeth sat up straight in her chair and leaned toward her friend. "What did Robert say?"

"He said the men like Major Caldwell just fine. They wish they had his way with women, but he ain't never dirtied anyone's reputation."

"I guess that's good news." Elizabeth eased back in her chair.

Mary Lee let out a sigh of relief. "It was to me. I asked Robert 'cause I was right worried when I saw you was gettin' interested."

Elizabeth took comfort in Mary Lee's words. She pushed her teacup aside. "Let's get started on this list. I think you'll find that it will all fall into place. I'll read your leaves while you go over the list."

Elizabeth examined the cup with great care before she said, "Come stand behind me. We'll look at the leaves together."

Mary Lee did as she was bid.

Elizabeth began. "Now, see here? This indicates people; some are busy and some standing in small groups. Up here, it looks like the sun. Guess it's going to be a pretty day for your wedding. And look down here. What does that look like to you?"

Mary Lee turned her head this way and that. "Nothin'. A bunch of wet tealeaves?"

"No. It looks like a package tied with a string, and its coming from a distance."

"I swear, Miz' Elizabeth, I don't know how you see anythin' in that cup."

Elizabeth saw something else in that cup. She didn't tell her friend, but there was a dark cloud hanging over the wedding. Did it mean a rainy day or was it a bad omen?

She was not going to upset her friend. "Mary Lee, let's go over the wedding party first. Robert's brother is to be the best man, and his other brothers will be the ushers. Is that right?"

"That's right. Robert's already told 'em they have to wear suits. He said they fussed about it, but were goin' to do it just fer him."

"Loyal friends." Elizabeth grinned. "We'll cross that off the list."

"And, yer goin' to be the maid of honor."

"Yes. I have Irene Butler sewing a lace dress of soft pink. That will look coordinated with your cream colored lace. I didn't think we should mix materials."

"What about yer hat?"

"I thought we could fashion one from the pink material left over from the dress and trim it with narrow pink and cream satin ribbon. I want it to be simple and elegant at the same time. It will complement your dress. It will be your day to shine.

"I'm startin' to get excited. What about flowers?"

"That comes next," said Elizabeth. They were interrupted with a customer coming into the shop.

She pushed the list in front of Mary Lee. "Here, you look at the rest of this and tell me what you think."

The customer was Grace Hawthorne. Doctor Hawthorne had accepted an invitation to an affair in Winchester and failed to tell his wife.

"I swan, Elizabeth, if he gets any busier, he will have to ask another doctor to come and share his practice. He's gone all hours of the day and night."

Elizabeth nodded in agreement. "I guess that's what they mean by a doctor's wife being a doctor's widow."

"Sometimes I feel like it." Grace looked into the mirror and adjusted the hat she had picked out with Elizabeth's help. She bought matching satin elbow length gloves and a pair of earrings.

"You must be going to something fancy, Mrs. Hawthorne."

"We are going to a banquet and concert with two other couples."

"I would love to go."

"Your time will come, my dear," she said.

She called to the industrious Mary Lee, "I wish you well with your wedding next month. It will be here before you know it."

"Thank you, Miz' Hawthorne."

Grace was out the door with a satisfied look, and Elizabeth felt equally as pleased.

She went over to the counter where Mary Lee was busy checking off the list. "Well, what do you think?"

"Oh, Miz' Elizabeth. I don't think you've forgot anythin'. I hope this is goin' to be the grand day Robert wants."

And so do I Mary Lee, thought Elizabeth, as she attempted to push the dark cloud in the tealeaves out of her mind.

Chapter 25

The evening of May 7th was one of those dark nights when you can't see your hand in front of your face. Elizabeth brought out the copper ham boiler and put it on the stove in the kitchen. She was preparing to heat up water in the boiler to rinse out some soiled clothes when she heard a rap at her back door. The shop had been closed for two hours. Whoever it was, wasn't there for anything in the shop or they would have come to the front door.

She was hesitant to go down the stairs, but the rapping persisted. She steeled her nerves. Taking the kerosene lamp, she ventured down the dark stairway. At the bottom of the steps she called out, "Who's there?"

The answer was a rapidity of insistent rapping.

She swallowed hard and called out in a husky voice. "What do you want?"

Then came a tapping on the window and she heard a loud whisper, "Elizabeth it's Andrew. I didn't want to come to the front door."

"Andrew!" In her hurry to get to the door she almost dropped the lamp. She fumbled as she tried to pull the bolt. "Hold on, Andrew. I'll have this open in a second."

When the bolt slid free, he pushed the door open and gathered her into his arms, kicking the door closed behind him.

Neither of them spoke after a flurry of kisses and they just stood in each other's arms.

Elizabeth's heart was beating like a hammer and she could feel Andrew's keeping a matching pace. She tried to step back but he held her tight and murmured in her ear, "Elizabeth, we have to get married."

Finally, she pulled away. "Let me catch my breath. You frightened me out of my shoes! Why didn't you send word you were coming?"

"Sorry about that. Can we go upstairs?"

He followed behind as they mounted the stairway. "I had a sudden order to return and I was flown home in a cargo plane. It was the case of being in the right place at the right time. I can't say as it was comfortable sitting among the empty crates, but I was happy to land safely."

"But how did you get here? The trains aren't running at this time."

"No. I paid a cab driver handsomely to drive me all the way from D.C."

"But, weren't you supposed to go to the base?"

"They expect me to come by ship, so I'm a few days ahead of time."

She raised her eyebrows, "Won't you get into trouble?"

"Call it what you will," he kissed her cheek. "I'll be back when they expect me. Tonight

I'll stay at the hotel, and tomorrow we can get married, whether it's by a minister or a Justice of the Peace."

He was slimmer and his bright green eyes were tired, but he was still the same handsome soldier she had waved goodbye to almost two months ago.

"And, I have no say in this? Andrew, have you really thought this out?"

"All the way to England and back and all the days in between." He smiled and reached for her hand.

"I fully intend to get Matthew back. If I do, what is that going to do to your family? They will be shamed just like my parents were. That wouldn't be fair to them."

"Elizabeth, don't you think I've sorted all this out? We get married, and then we get Matthew. You've said that you want to move back to the city. You sell this shop and we'll settle in D.C."

She rose from the sofa and went to stand by the fireplace. "You make it sound so easy, but it won't be. Your family will be humiliated, and Ruth and I are already at odds. She would probably like nothing better than to have you marry a fallen woman so she can hang it over your head for the rest of your life."

He was off the sofa in a flash. "Don't talk like that! I don't care what my family or anyone else thinks. I love you as you are. So are you going to marry me or not?"

She shot back, "Yes I am!"

He stopped dead still. "You are?"

"I have mulled it over in my mind since the day you proposed on the sidewalk. At first, I thought you felt sorry for me. Then, when you went away, I went over and over the times we had spent together, and I knew you were sincere. If you could overlook the fact that I bore an illegitimate child, you must love me very much."

In one giant step he reached and drew her into his arms. "Elizabeth, I was so worried. All the time I was in England until I arrived tonight, I was so afraid you would say no."

She leaned into his chest feeling the comfort of his embrace. "I do care deeply for you, Andrew. If we can weather the storms that lie ahead, we can build a strong union."

"Let's make a pact," he said. "We will meet whatever comes, together, and forget those who try to give us grief. If we have real friends, they will stick with us."

She tipped her head back to look up at him, "I hope you're right. Would you like something to eat?"

"Not just now." he kissed her forehead. "I'm going over to the hotel. The cab driver is bedded down there, and, in the morning, we will be on our way to Washington to get married by either a preacher or Justice of the Peace."

"We couldn't possibly do that."

"Why not?"

"Because I have a shop to run, and because I'll lose money."

"Where's your adventurous side, Elizabeth? For me it was a do or die proposition. I've made arrangements with Asa to find a preacher so we can be married at five o'clock tomorrow. He and Carolyn will stand up with us. We'll have a feast at the Willard, and I have the best suite reserved."

She stood back, hands on hips. "Quite sure of yourself, aren't you, Andrew? What if I had said no? And, what if I don't want Asa and Carolyn standing up with us, and, what if I don't want to stay at the Willard?"

"You don't want to stay at the Willard?" he teased.

"I wish I had a new dress," she lamented.

"We'll buy one in Washington."

"I won't be able to sleep a wink."

He gave her a warm smile, "And, neither will I. Won't we be a handsome pair when we stand before whoever the preacher turns out to be?"

"What time are we leaving?"

"Seven in the morning, sharp."

"Yes sir," she said with mock salute. "I shall be packed and ready."

He gave her a full-bodied kiss on the lips and she returned his fervor.

"Now, I have to pull myself away and get over to the hotel, or we could stay in your bedroom."

She shook her head. "You do have a mischievous side. That's wishful thinking on your part."

"You can't say I didn't try. I'll go out the back door so you'll have to bolt it behind me."

"No, Andrew," she answered. "Go out the front door. "Let's really give Lavinia something to talk about!"

"You're absolutely right." He tapped the tip of her nose with his finger. "I'll press the lock when I leave. I love you, Elizabeth."

"And, I can say with all honesty, that I love you, Andrew. Just think, tomorrow evening at this time I will be Mrs. Andrew Caldwell."

"And, I will be sporting a wife on my arm at the Willard." He gave her a quick kiss, hustled down the front stairs, turned the lock and was out the door.

Elizabeth smiled to herself as she watched the door close. Was it the hand of Providence that had delivered Andrew? It mattered not. Tomorrow, Elizabeth Fairchilds was going to marry the love of her life!

****

The next morning, Elizabeth was ready and so nervous she could hardly write. She scribbled off a note to Mary Lee telling her that Andrew came home, and they were going to Washington to be married. Mary Lee could open the shop if she wanted, but she was to keep Elizabeth's wedding a secret. Although Elizabeth knew the news would throw her friend into a tizzy, it couldn't be helped. She stuck the tightly sealed envelope with Mary Lee's name on it in the window of the front door of the shop, where it wouldn't blow off.

231

The cab pulled in front of her place and Andrew jumped out. He lifted her suitcase as though it was filled with down. He stashed it in the front with the driver before he helped her into the back seat.

After they were seated and on their way, he addressed the driver, "This is my wife to be, Miss Fairchilds. Elizabeth, meet Hank."

"Proud to meet you, ma'am," Hank answered without turning from the wheel. "Major Caldwell talked about you all the way from D.C. last night, and I can see why. You pretty up my cab."

Andrew squeezed her hand, and Elizabeth flushed an attractive pink.

Andrew was relaxed and napped most of the ride back. Elizabeth was on alert. Questions and uncertainty whirled around in her head. She thought of her parents' reaction. Then Mary Lee popped into her mind. Oh my, what about Mary Lee? Could her action of taking off on a whim of the moment be the cloud hanging over Mary Lee's wedding? Elizabeth closed her eyes, which did nothing to allay her thoughts.

Once they reached the city, she felt more peaceful. The driver stopped in front of the city hall where they were to get the marriage license. Andrew paid him what must have been more money than Elizabeth wanted to think about, because Hank flashed a grin from ear to ear and said, " Anytime you need me, you just call."

Elizabeth stood looking at the large stone building. "Andrew, I feel like I'll be signing my life away."

He took her arm, "No, my love, our lives are just beginning!"

Friday was a busy day in the city hall. They waited on a bench for a half hour before they received the paperwork. Then they filled in the information and waited another half hour before they could see the registrar. He had apologized for the delay but attributed it to many couples rushing their marriage because of the war.

The war! Elizabeth hadn't considered that fact. "Andrew, is the war the reason you're pushing marriage?"

"Of course not." With license in hand, he said, "I will have to call Asa to see what he has lined up. But first, I'm going to take you to a dress shop. While you're shopping, I'll make the call and you won't have to be concerned about me being in the way."

As they walked from the city hall down a street of fine shops, Elizabeth was beginning to doubt her actions. "Andrew, what if you're shipped off to Europe? Perhaps we should wait."

"Wait for what? We never know what tomorrow will bring so we must enjoy each day as it comes."

They came to a little shop she had shopped in before. It was more expensive but that fact did not deter her.

Andrew kissed her cheek. "I'll be back in about thirty minutes."

Elizabeth entered the shop and was distracted by the lovely displays.

"Good morning, miss."

"Good morning."

"Why, Miss Fairchilds, isn't it?" asked the matronly saleslady. She wore a pair of reading glasses on a fancy chain around her neck. They perched on her prominent bosom.

"Yes," answered Elizabeth with a confused look.

"You were in a couple of years ago. How could I forget a pretty face like yours? You bought a dress for a dance you were going to at school. A yellow satin, if I remember correctly."

What a memory this woman has, thought Elizabeth. "Yes, ma'am, and I still have it."

"What can I do for you today?"

"I am looking for another dress for a special occasion."

"How fortunate you have come in today when we received a shipment of the latest fashions yesterday. Any special color in mind?"

"I need something in the light shades like ecru, cream or beige."

The lady clasped her hands together. "Perfect for this time of year. Come right this way. Have a chair and I'll bring out the ones we have. Keep in mind that our seamstress can make any alterations needed."

"I am in a bit of a hurry. I'm not sure I can wait for alterations."

"I'll show you what we have and we can work from there."

The kindly saleslady appeared with five dresses in hand. "I'm afraid we are limited in the new selection, so I brought two of last year's. They are still stylish. In fact, better made. The war effort is shortening the skirts and lessening the quality of the material."

Of the five the woman displayed, there was one that caught Elizabeth's eye. "I would like to try the cream."

"Of course, what a good choice. May I ask what kind of an affair you're attending?"

"My wedding." Elizabeth checked her watch. "In just about four hours."

If the answer was a shock to the large woman, she never missed a beat. "And, you're not wanting a white wedding dress? We have several."

"The war has dampened many plans. We might even be getting married by a Justice of the Peace so I think a wedding gown is out of the question."

"Quite right you are. Let's try this one and see what we have."

Elizabeth slipped into the dress and the saleslady hooked it up.

"Come over here and look in the full length mirror."

Elizabeth looked at her reflection in the glass and caught her breath. "It's beautiful."

"Pure silk. I must confess that it is a copy of one from the French designer, Doucet. Notice how the chiffon overlay shimmers when you move. It's last year's model, but it has the popular embroidered v-neckline with this striking camisole underneath. It looks lovely on your small trim figure."

"I hesitate to ask the price."

The saleslady took a moment before she replied. "I think I should have Gladys shorten the underskirt to calf length. Once that's done, I can let it go for thirty-five dollars."

Elizabeth's heart sank. She had thirty dollars in her purse. The lady must have seen the look of disappointment on Elizabeth's face because she added, "Of course, as I said, its last year's dress. I could take thirty."

"Would that include the shortening?"

"Certainly, Gladys can zip that up in a few minutes."

"I'll take it."

"A perfect choice," answered the saleslady as she sang out, "Gla…dys,".

A bent, wrinkled, little lady came to the door.

"We need this dress shortened right away."

"Yes, ma'am." She set down her sewing basket, motioned for Elizabeth to step up onto a square box, and began tucking up the hem with straight pins. "This is the length that everyone tells us we need this year. Does this suit?" she asked.

"That will be fine."

Gladys helped Elizabeth remove the dress and slid out the door, dress in hand. "Wait here."

Elizabeth did as she was told feeling a bit embarrassed sitting in her underpinnings.

But it couldn't have been fifteen minutes before the seamstress returned with the shortened dress and the hem pressed.

She motioned for Elizabeth to stand before the mirror, which the bride-to-be didn't question. Gladys pulled the dress over her head and fastened the back fussing around pulling down the underskirt, straightening the neckline and pulling down the long sleeves of the camisole.

"You work fast," said Elizabeth trying to make conversation.

"I've been doing this for thirty years. You look pretty as a picture. I hear it's your wedding day."

"At five o'clock, if all goes according to plan."

"I hope you picked a good one. I got married once, which was a mistake and that's why I've been doing this kind of work since."

The woman's words did nothing to quell the flip-flops already doing somersaults in Elizabeth's stomach. She turned to survey the back of the dress. "I'm sorry to hear that."

Gladys unhooked the dress and helped Elizabeth into her street clothes. Then she left the room with the wedding dress slung over her arm.

At the counter the saleswoman carefully folded the dress before she placed it into a dress box. "I had hoped to see the finished product on you, but I was busy with a customer and I know you are pushed for time."

Just then, Andrew walked in the door. The woman looked up, and whispered. "Is this your young man?"

Elizabeth gave her a warm smile. "Yes."

"Such a handsome one. You are a lucky girl."

Andrew came up to the counter and flashed the woman a winning smile. "What an attractive shop you have here."

The woman was almost giddy. "Thank you, sir."

Elizabeth smiled to herself. The charming Major Caldwell had done it again.

"Did you find what you were looking for?" he asked Elizabeth.

"I am pleased." She reached into her pocket-book when Andrew stayed her hand.

"Let me pay for it."

"No, Andrew. I want to pay for this myself."

Elizabeth counted out her hard-earned money. It was a rite of passage, a badge of honor that she had painfully acquired over the past year.

"Good luck to you," the saleslady called as they exited the shop.

Andrew flagged down a taxi. He gave the driver an address in Georgetown.

"Georgetown?" Elizabeth questioned. "I need to get back to the hotel to change."

"Catherine and Patrick will be at the wedding and they have opened the house for what we need until the ceremony."

Her eyes opened wide. "They are coming to the wedding? I don't even know them that well."

"They will be there with Asa and Carolyn. Asa's made the arrangements."

A pang of anxiety crept into her voice. "Andrew I thought it would just be you and me in front of a magistrate."

He kissed her hand. "We have to have witnesses."

"Do you realize how unnerved I am?"

"We both are."

She offered a weak smile. "Perhaps, but you don't show it."

He pointed to his heart. "It's all in here. I will be giving up the undeserved label of being a ladies' man."

That announcement brought a laugh. "You may not realize it, but you do have a way of making a lady feel special, no matter what her age. I admire that gift as long as you remember that you belong to this lady."

The taxi pulled to the side of the street in front of the Burkes' red brick, colonial home.

Carolyn came bursting out the door and down the walk. "We have been worried that you weren't going to make it. Andrew, Asa and Patrick are waiting in the library. Elizabeth, come with me."

They followed Carolyn up the walk and into the house. Catherine was waiting in an upstairs bedroom and came to the head of the stairs to greet Elizabeth.

"I didn't realize the time," said Elizabeth. "I have my dress here in this box. I hope it isn't too wrinkled."

Catherine offered, "Mattie can do a quick press, if need be. We've been holding our breath waiting to see it."

Elizabeth placed the box on top of the bed and carefully lifted the dress from its resting place.

Carolyn took it from her hands and danced around the bed. "Oh, Elizabeth, its beautiful."

"It is that," agreed Catherine. "Neither Carolyn nor I would be able to fit into it. Do you have a headpiece?"

Elizabeth was honest. "I spent all of my money on the dress."

"Good," said Catherine. "I fashioned something that I thought would go with any material. Would you like to see it?"

"I'd be delighted," answered Elizabeth, pleased at the prospect of gaining a piece to complete her outfit.

Catherine disappeared into an adjoining room and returned with a brimless, silk, ecru-colored hat with white seed pearls fashionably sewed into the crown. A delicate white feather curled from the side of the hat.

Catherine placed it on her head. "It is my wedding gift to you, if you approve."

Elizabeth was overjoyed with her reflection in the mirror. "How perfect. I can't thank you enough, Catherine."

Carolyn brought them back to the task at hand. "Any thanks will have to be quick, we're behind time."

At that pronouncement, all three became a whirlwind of activity at getting Elizabeth dressed and ready for the biggest step in her life.

Chapter 26

The next morning Elizabeth and Andrew, entwined like a braid, awoke on a down mattress at the Willard. As he promised, it was the best suite in the hotel.

"I apologize for not giving you the wedding you deserve," he said as he nuzzled her warm neck.

"Andrew, it couldn't have been more perfect. Do you realize what we crammed into a matter of hours?"

"Unfortunately, yes. That's why I feel guilty. But, I will make it up to you."

She kissed his cheek and ran her fingers through his thick auburn hair. "And what would you have wanted differently?" she asked.

"Not for me, but for you."

"I was pleased and proud of the whole affair. All the insignificant worries I had were washed away. You had better thank Asa for the preparations he made at the last minute."

He laughed. "I'm sure Asa didn't have that much to do. He's a master at giving orders so he probably turned it over to Carolyn. Then she got together with Catherine and the ladies planned the whole thing. Patrick said Catherine was in her glory when she heard we were to be married in the same little church in Georgetown where they were married. She insisted on making your headpiece."

Elizabeth snuggled closer under the cradle of his arm. "It was kind of Catherine and Patrick to open their home to us before the wedding. There I was in Catherine's bedroom with her and Carolyn dressing me. I didn't have time to think. Carolyn dabbed some Elizabeth Arden makeup on my face, which, by the way, she said is all the rage. Then the three of us piled into a cab, went to the church, the preacher's wife thrust a bouquet of roses at me, and I was walking down the aisle. It seems like a dream. If it is, don't wake me up because here we are and I never want to move."

He kissed her forehead. "And neither do I, but we do have to eat."

"After all that food we had last night? We still have some of the wedding cake over on the dresser. We can eat that for breakfast."

"You are all the sweets in the morning that I can handle, my love. How do you feel?"

"The happiest I have ever been in my life. I'm afraid to get out of bed because I think my happiness bubble will burst. Besides, I don't think I dare get out of bed with this nightgown I'm wearing."

His admiration showed in a wide grin. "It leaves little to the imagination."

"I would think Carolyn would have been embarrassed to buy it. It's positively sinful."

He ran his hand down her side. "But, you're wearing it so it is positively perfect." He threw the covers to the side. "As much as I'd like to not move an inch, we have matters that need our attention."

She traced her fingers up his bare chest. "We must have fifteen minutes we can spare," she teased.

He pulled her close. "Where's that stand-offish lass I once knew?"

"Gone. She's gone forever, deliriously pleased with her choice in a husband."

Twenty minutes later they were getting dressed for the day with Andrew whistling and Elizabeth humming to herself. She interrupted him to ask, "Do you think we have time to visit my parents?"

"I wondered when you were going to suggest that. You said you've mended the fence. How do you think they will receive the news of our marriage?"

Elizabeth sat on the bed beside him where he was pulling on his long socks. "I'm not sure. I'd hate to have it set Mother off. We do have to tell them."

"Let's enjoy today. Tomorrow is Sunday. Perhaps we can visit in the afternoon."

"When do you have to be back at the base?"

"According to Asa, they are expecting me to arrive Tuesday evening."

She slid her hand through his arm. "I wish it was never. I'll call today and see if my parents are up to us coming. We can break the news together."

Andrew patted her hand. "This will all work out. Let's not concern ourselves with it today. Tomorrow will be soon enough."

She leaned her head on his shoulder. "I pray you're right. I'll try not to worry, but I've had some go-rounds with my parents and I'm not looking forward to another."

"And, neither am I. We shall be gracious, accommodating and state our case before they boot us out the door."

Elizabeth laughed. "How can you be so easy?"

"Practice, my love. It's a cruel world out there." He stood up and offered his hand. "Now, we must get something to eat because I am famished."

She took his hand. "Not before you kiss me once more before we go."

With a flourish, he lifted her off her feet and kissed her with gusto. "Will that do?" he asked as he set her feet back onto the floor.

"That was more than satisfactory," she answered. "I'm ready for the day."

****

Because it was such a lovely May day, they spent most of it outdoors taking in the sights of Washington. It seemed every corner had a building going up or one coming down. They found a quiet little restaurant where they sat out on the sidewalk and watched the populace hurry by.

"I miss the bustle of the city, Andrew. It seems as though every time I come there is something new to see. The people have places to go and things to do, unlike my existence in Berryville."

"Washington is busy, but it still seems like a dirty city to me," he replied. "There's always dust in the air, mud in the street and unclean dampness in the air. That's why I get out to Red Gate as often as I can."

She was sipping tea and eating an egg sandwich. "I understand, but here you can walk in the park or sit by the restful river. I miss the theatres, the museums, the concerts…"

"Which I have tickets for this evening," he said. "It's not a name orchestra but I've heard them before. They play everything from Beethoven to ragtime with waltzes and marches thrown in."

She gave him a bright, happy smile. "I can hardly wait. Aren't I the luckiest woman in the whole world?"

He chuckled. "That's rather a broad statement, but keep that thought in mind."

Even the phone call Elizabeth had made earlier to Mary Lee had gone well. In her own true-blue way she had said, 'Don't you fret 'bout a thing, Miz' Elizabeth. I'll just open the shop and do my best 'til you get back.'

Any worries Elizabeth had about leaving the hat shop unattended had been allayed.

The newlyweds spent the whole afternoon and evening in pleasant conversation. Neither of them mentioned the war, the fate of her child, or the impending visit with her parents on Sunday.

The concert was at seven. They returned to their room in time to dress for the evening's entertainment.

Elizabeth lamented her sparse choice of attire. "You are so lucky, Andrew. You just have to spruce up your uniform. Never a care as to what you will wear."

"One of the benefits of being in the cavalry," he said. "Besides, it gives me time to admire watching you climb into your clothes. You do look fetching when you finish."

She gave him a kiss as she passed by to sit before the dressing mirror.

Once they left the hotel, they ate at a fine restaurant before taking a cab to the theatre. It was an hour and a half of music with small comedic skits mixed in. Elizabeth clapped and clapped and clapped. They arrived back at the Willard around ten o'clock where they fell exhausted onto the soft, beckoning bed.

It was the middle of the night when Elizabeth shouted out and sat up with a start. She was trembling and crying.

Andrew awoke immediately and threw his arms around her. "My God, Elizabeth, what's wrong?"

She shook her head as though trying to rid it of the nightmare. "I dreamed you were off to war and lay dying. You were all alone...no one was there but you with your life pouring out. It was so real...so frightening."

He soothed her until she quieted. "I'm right here with no plans to leave."

"But, you could go. It's on my mind more and more."

"Yes, I could go, but no troops have been sent. Our first concern is meeting your parents tomorrow. We can only meet one crisis at a time." He gave her a gentle kiss before she settled back down.

"We'll be a sorry looking pair if we don't get some sleep. No more bad dreams. We have an interesting day ahead of us."

****

The next afternoon she and Andrew took the trolley from Washington to Alexandria. They walked the two blocks to the large white house where Elizabeth was born. Mounting the wide set of steps, they climbed to the porch. She rang the bell.

"Are you concerned about meeting my parents, Andrew?"

He smiled at her. "No. It might be unpleasant, but we will weather the storm, if it comes to that. They are as interested in keeping you and getting Matthew back as we are so I don't expect they are going to throw us out on our ears. Besides, what would the neighbors say?"

"I don't know how you can treat this so lightly."

He put his arm around her waist and squeezed. "It will be fine."

She sighed, "I hope you're right."

Opal opened the door.

"Miz' Elizabeth. How good to see you. Come in. Your parents are in the parlor waiting for you."

Elizabeth put her finger to her lips before whispering in Opal's ear, "This is my husband, Andrew."

Opal rolled her eyes toward heaven and took a deep sigh before she led them to her parents.

Francis Fairchilds rose from his chair to greet them.

"Father, this is Major Andrew Caldwell. I told you I would be bringing a guest."

"Of course. It's a pleasure to meet you, Major. I'm pleased to present my wife."

Gertrude Fairchilds remained seated.

Andrew took a stride forward and took her hand. "Mrs. Fairchilds, I am honored."

She offered a slight nod and a dispirited smile.

Elizabeth's father motioned for them to take a seat. "Would you care for some refreshment before dinner?"

They declined and took their seats side by side on the stiff horsehair sofa.

"We were surprised to hear from you, Elizabeth. I believe we agreed you would stay in Berryville until I called."

"I'm sorry, Father. I realize this is unexpected," Elizabeth began, "but Andrew has just returned from England." She wasn't sure how to say the next words so she stated them plainly, "We were married Friday."

Neither parent spoke, while an uncomfortable silence followed. Once the news had settled in, Francis cleared his throat and Gertrude turned away with a disgruntled look. Elizabeth squirmed in her seat.

Andrew was the first to speak, "I apologize for not giving Elizabeth the proper wedding, but the army's time is not always in step with the rest of the world."

Francis emptied the ashes from the bowl of his pipe with a noticeable thud. "This is highly unusual and quite unacceptable. Elizabeth has given us no indication that she had a steady suitor much less jumping into a marriage with someone we have never met."

Andrew countered, "For that I apologize. We have known each other for the past eight months."

"Nonetheless, sir. This should have been handled differently."

The words caused Elizabeth to bristle. "You don't know how difficult it has been for me to come here. I had hoped you would be pleased, relieved even…"

Andrew took her hand as a caution to maintain her calm.

Gertrude Fairchilds finally turned to face them. "We should be pleased? You come in and casually drop the news that you had a hasty wedding to someone we have never met, never gave us the courtesy of an invitation, and we're to rejoice?

Have you been honest with him, Elizabeth?" She ignored Andrew as though he didn't exist.

Andrew wouldn't be ignored. "Certainly she has. Do you think you raised a dishonest daughter?"

Elizabeth was startled by his brusque reply, but pleased he had come to her defense. Her throat felt constricted, preventing her from saying a word.

Andrew took the lead, "We are sorry if it appears we were inconsiderate. We will not apologize for our decision to wed. We want you to be pleased about our union, but if that is unpardonable, then so be it. I am well aware of the situation with Matthew, and we hope to work together to get him back."

This must have struck a note in Francis because his tone was appeasing, "You must realize we were taken aback by your announcement. If you are both satisfied, then we will learn to accept it."

"What do you say, Mother?" asked Elizabeth.

"All I have ever wanted for you is to have a good life. What's done is done. I don't know how one child can give a mother such pain."

Andrew rose and went to Elizabeth's mother, who was close to tears. He took her hand. "I understand how you both feel. I will do the best I can for your daughter, and I would like nothing better than to have you accept me as your son-in-law."

Gertrude nodded her bowed head.

251

Francis broke the tension. "I think we can all do with a stout glass of wine and some food. Opal has been keeping dinner warm. Shall we go into the dining room?"

Dinner began with quiet politeness and conversation warmed up as the meal progressed, although there were no congratulatory toasts. Andrew filled Elizabeth's parents in on his life's story, which seemed to relax both parents. Eventually the subject of Matthew came up.

"Your marriage does change the situation. I don't know if that will be helpful or frowned upon," said her father.

Elizabeth sounded hopeful as she questioned, "Do you think if we talked to the priest in charge he could still make the decision rather than have it go to the bishop? You said he was in favor of rescinding the adoption order. Maybe being a married couple will be favorable."

"A possibility," said her father. "I'm sure this is only going to the bishop because the nun at the orphanage and the priest are at odds. Mostly, I suspect it's because of the status of the adoptive couple. I understand they are not only influential in Washington, but they donate heavily to Catholic institutions."

Gertrude had been listening until then. "Why don't you call the lawyer in the morning, Francis?" she suggested. "Perhaps he can make arrangements for all of us to meet with the priest and the nun together?"

"That sounds like the exact plan," said Andrew, which brought a pleasurable smile from Gertrude.

Francis mulled it over. "I'll call as soon as the office opens and see what he can do."

The lady of the house rang a small crystal bell summoning Opal to clear away the dinner dishes.

Once she had cleared the table, she returned with a chocolate pie topped with whipped cream for dessert.

Andrew flashed his engaging smile. "Opal that is the fanciest pie I've ever seen. If it tastes as good as it looks, you shall be named the Queen of Pies."

There was a visible blush under the maid's dusky skin.

Elizabeth sat admiring her husband working his winning ways with the women in the house.

Before they left, her father drew her aside. "Elizabeth, I have been observing the two of you together all afternoon and I am pleased to see a mutual love and respect. You seem to have made a good choice."

"Thank you, Father. I do believe the Lord was smiling down on me when he sent Andrew."

Chapter 27

Francis Fairchilds walked into the reception area of Jacob Cunningham's office, much to the surprise of the male secretary.

"Good morning, sir. May I be of assistance?"

"Sorry I'm here without an appointment. Is Jacob in? I have pressing business."

"He is in, but I will have to see if he is available."

The male secretary disappeared into the lawyer's office only to return with Jacob at his heels.

"Come in, Francis. It must be urgent to have you here this early."

"It is that," replied the anxious Francis. They went into the office where he took a chair facing the portly lawyer.

"Elizabeth is married. She and her husband came by yesterday. The four of us would like to have an audience with the nun from the orphanage and the priest you've dealt with preferably by tomorrow morning or afternoon."

"Whoa, Francis," came Jacob's reply, as he threw up his hands. "How do you propose I do that?"

"Lawyers have their ways," Francis shot him a cunning look. "Elizabeth's husband is of solid stock, family lives across the Blue Ridge on a big estate. He's a major in the army and as eager to have Matthew with them as we are."

The chair squeaked under Jacob's ample weight. "What do you propose I do, tell the priest that he doesn't have to bother the bishop because we have the whole problem solved?"

"That would be nice, if it would work," encouraged Francis; pleased the lawyer was giving it some thought.

Jacob rose and paced around the room before he resumed his seat behind the desk. "You never told me Elizabeth would be married."

"It was a rushed affair."

Jacob cocked an eyebrow. "Another problem?"

Francis gave him a dour look. "No. In fact, I like the chap. Of course, her mother and I would have preferred to have had it happen in a more acceptable way, but that is not the case."

Jacob rubbed his sideburns as if in thought. "Let me do this. I'll put in a call to Father Joseph who has handled this whole debacle. Perhaps he can work something out. If he and that nun had agreed, we'd have been out of this mess weeks ago."

"I couldn't ask for more," said the relieved Francis. "Thank you for being so kind." He shook the lawyer's hand.

"You'll be getting my bill," kidded the lawyer as he opened the door. "I'll call you this afternoon one way or another."

Francis spent an anxiety filled day until Jacob's call came around four-thirty in the afternoon.

"Francis? This is Jacob. Here is the best I can do. The priest said his hands are tied. The four of you have an audience with the bishop at eight o'clock next Friday morning."

"But, I'm not sure all four of us can make it."

"My advice is the four of you had better show up if you have any chance of reversing that adoption request!"

"I understand. Thank you." He hung up the phone, sank his slim body into a nearby chair, and was in deep thought when his wife came into the room.

"I heard the phone ring. Not good news?"

"A bit of trouble, Gertie. The four of us need to meet with the bishop next Friday morning. Jacob said that it is imperative."

She gave him a weak smile. "Then there is no question. The four of us will have to be there."

"What if Andrew can't get the time?"

"Then the three of us will have to convince this bishop that Matthew's rightful place is with his family." She walked over and kissed the top of his head. "Come. Opal has our meal ready."

****

Elizabeth returned to Berryville to find disaster in the form of Mary Lee.

There had been a fire around the altar in the Presbyterian church, where she and Robert were to be married, and it would be a couple of months before it would be usable.

She was sobbing away. "I jus' don' know what we're gonna' do."

Elizabeth had her own troubles. She didn't need another one. Her doleful friend looked so pitiful it wrenched her heart. "There are other churches, Mary Lee. Perhaps the wedding can take place in one of them."

"I wouldn't feel right in any other church. Robert says maybe we should forgit the whole thing and go to a justice of the peace. He said there's no way he's gonna' change the weddin' date. He's got time off from the farm and everythin'." The words caused her to boohoo all the louder.

While Elizabeth was consoling her friend, an idea flashed through her mind. "Why not have the wedding in my backyard? You can have the minister marry you in the gazebo."

Mary Lee brightened at the thought, but not without doubt. "I don't know 'bout that. Do you think the preacher would do that?"

"You can ask him. I'm sure he feels as badly about the fire as you do."

"But, what if it rains?"

"It's not going to rain. Don't you remember the big sun shining the last time I read your tealeaves?" Elizabeth had never told Mary Lee about the time she saw the dark cloud she had seen another day. She certainly wouldn't tell her now. "I'll bet the minister will let us borrow tables and chairs from the church."

Mary Lee's blue eyes were beginning to look less puffy. "Oh, Miz' Elizabeth. Do you think so?"

"I'll bet he'd be more than happy to."

Enthused, Mary Lee suggested that Robert could get help to haul the tables and chairs with a farm wagon.

Mary Lee's unhappy mood was noticeably improved.

Later that day, Elizabeth got a call from her father about the eight o'clock meeting on Friday, which meant she had to make preparations for the return to Washington. She recalled the words of Shakespeare, 'When troubles come, they come not single fold, but in battalions.'

Lavinia Talley picked that morning to propel herself into the shop, while Elizabeth and Mary Lee were busy finalizing wedding plans pending the minister's agreement to use the backyard gazebo.

Lavinia was gushing. "My goodness, Elizabeth. You've missed all the excitement. And, poor Mary Lee here." She cast a doubtful eye at the already jittery bride-to-be. "Whatever will you do about a wedding now? It just wasn't meant to be, that's all there is to it."

"Wal' Miz' Elizabeth says…"

Elizabeth raised her hand to quiet her friend. "You never know about weddings, Mrs. Talley. Why just four days ago Andrew Caldwell and I were married in Washington."

Lavinia almost swooned. The news was more than she could bear. She was speechless. Like corn mash ferments into billowing foam, she blew out of the shop to explode with the news.

With regret, Elizabeth had to tell Mary Lee that she had to make another trip to Washington on Thursday. "Now, if you can't watch the shop, I'll just close it down. I know you're already up in the air with your wedding around the corner and the mess we're in with that."

"I know you wouldn't go if it wasn't important. I got lotsa nit-picky things to keep me busy. When are you comin' back?"

"I will have to see how this meeting goes on Friday morning and go from there."

"Sounds mighty important."

"I'd like to tell you the reason, but for now, I can't. I promise I will tell you all about it when I return."

****

Thursday evening Francis Fairchilds went to the Alexandria station to meet Elizabeth.

He gave his daughter a welcome hug. "Did you have a good ride in?"

"Train rides are never comfortable," she replied. "Has Andrew called?"

"He has," said her father as he picked up her tapestry satchel. "He hopes to get to the house by ten o'clock. He said there was no need to wait up." He gave his daughter a wink. "I'm sure he meant your mother and I."

Elizabeth grinned. "What is the mood at home? Has Mother forgiven me for my impetuous marriage?"

259

"We both forgave you that very day. Andrew is a fine person. It isn't easy to win your mother's heart, but I believe he has done that."

"I put the shop up for sale this week. Now that my helper is getting married, she'll be secure so I don't have to feel concern for her. I want to get on with my life."

They had reached the car and he held the door as she stepped up on the running board.

"I'm happy to hear you're getting rid of that shop. I hope you will have a quick response from someone wanting to buy."

"I can't sell it before my friend, Mary Lee, is married in my backyard."

"Is that unexpected?"

"Not the marriage, but the setting," she answered. "There was a fire in the church while I was away. The crew from the fire company put it out, but not before there was extensive damage to the altar. Her minister has agreed to the outdoor wedding, and he offered to let her borrow tables and chairs from the church."

"Generous of him," said her father. The1915 Ford puttered along.

On the way home, Elizabeth put her thoughts into words. "You know, Father, I bore hard feelings against you and Mother for sending me away. But, if I am honest with myself, I believe it was the right move. I had a lot of growing up to do."

"And, you grew up beautifully, Lizzie. It was painful to all of us. Let's put it behind and meet what comes ahead."

Forgiveness is such a satisfied feeling. Elizabeth let out a sigh of relief.

When they reached the house, they found Andrew and Gertrude chatting in the parlor.

Andrew rose immediately, shook his father-in-law's hand and gave Elizabeth a warm embrace.

It was all she could do to restrain herself from wrapping herself up in her husband's arms. Instead she kissed his cheek and squeezed his hand. "Father said you would be coming later."

"Quite unexpected. Asa is covering for me. He's got the number here in case there's an emergency."

Elizabeth went to her mother and gave her a hug. "Hello, Mother."

Gertrude patted her daughter's hand. "Andrew and I have had a pleasant conversation. He's invited your father and me to come out to Red Gate Farm to meet his family."

"A wonderful idea," agreed Francis.

Elizabeth wasn't so sure. She changed the subject. "I'm hungry. Do you think Opal has left any dessert in the kitchen?"

"Opal always leaves dessert in the kitchen." Her Father chuckled as he cast an eye in his chunky wife's direction.

"Ignore your father," Gertrude said. "You two go ahead. It's time for us to retire. You and Andrew will be occupying your room, Elizabeth."

The thought of snuggling into her familiar bed brought a smile. "Thank you. What time must we leave in the morning?"

Her father spoke up. "I've ordered the taxi to be here at seven. That will allow us some time for any unforeseeable delay."

"You're not driving?" asked Elizabeth.

"I considered the taxi a better option."

Elizabeth smiled to herself. Was this the man who bought a tin-lizzy so he wouldn't have to pay the taxi and trolley fares?

As soon as Elizabeth's parents retired to their room, Andrew pulled Elizabeth into his arms.

"It's time for a proper welcome, Mrs. Caldwell," he said and planted an amorous kiss smack on her lips. After a few delicious seconds he released her. "You don't know how I've missed you."

"As I have you," she answered. "Let's eat and go straight to my room. I'm sure you won't mind sleeping in a canopied bed in a room with tiny pink flowers on the wallpaper."

"My dear, if you are in the bed, I don't care where I sleep." He brushed back golden hair and kissed her forehead.

****

The next morning Opal had prepared oatmeal, biscuits, boiled eggs and fried bacon to send the foursome off with a hearty breakfast. Elizabeth's stomach was in knots. She nibbled on a biscuit, ate half an egg and drank a cup of tea.

There seemed to be no impairment of appetite in the other three. Was she the only one a bundle of nerves over the coming meeting? She didn't have time to mull it over because the taxi was at the curb and waiting at five minutes before seven.

"I expressly said seven," her father remarked. "I'll not pay for an extra five minutes. Just more money for his coffers."

"You'll pay it, Francis, The poor man was undoubtedly afraid of the consequences if he was one minute late."

"Poor man, hah!" Francis huffed. "They've started that National Association of Taxi Owners just like they've got in Chicago. Mark my words, we'll be paying for it."

Gertrude Fairchilds voice was mollifying. "I don't blame them, dear. The government wants to take five percent of their receipts."

"What is this world coming to?" he grumbled.

All four scrambled to take a last glimpse in the hallway mirror before heading out to the waiting cab.

Andrew sat in front next to the driver after he and Francis navigated Gertrude onto the running board and into the back seat. She sat between her husband and daughter, squeezing them into the sides of the car.

It was a forty-five minute ride to the bishop's place. A young seminarian met them at the gate. Apparently they were expected because he asked, "The Fairchilds?"

They nodded. He led them along a path, under huge oak trees, where a large, limestone, Gothic-styled building loomed before them.

263

Elizabeth slid her arm through Andrew's and moved close to him.

"This is intimidating," she whispered.

"It's just a big house," he whispered back.

Their silent leader smiled at the exchange. He led them into a large vestibule with a high ceiling and stained glass windows, where he motioned to them to take a seat. No one said a word; they just exchanged worried glances. All they heard was the scuffing of branches as the stiff breeze outside caused them to brush against the windows.

The seminarian went into a side door. He returned a few minutes later and, in a voice barely above a whisper, said, "The bishop will see you now."

They entered into a large room where the bishop stood on a platform one step up from the floor. The four about to have an audience with the bishop stood like stones. There were three priests at different stations in the large office.

The bishop wore a violet zucchetto on his head and a black cassock trimmed with the same color violet. A pectoral cross hung around his neck. He gave a slight raise of his hand after he had scrutinized the party before him, and one of the priests showed them to four chairs placed around a u-shaped table. To the surprise of the four seated, the bishop came off the elevated station and sat with them at the table.

Another priest was quick to place a two-inch thick folder before the revered man who had not yet uttered a sound. He shuffled through the papers. When he seemed satisfied, he smiled at the four before him and said, "Ah yes, Matthew. He's caused quite a stir."

There was a shared inaudible sigh among the four. The man is human after all.

"My understanding is that this little tot is to be adopted and you have changed your minds."

Francis was the first to speak. "Yes sir. That's correct. Mrs. Fairchilds and I signed the papers in haste. When he was born, the doctor said he held little hope for our daughter's survival. We thought it was the best we could do for the child."

"I am also informed, this child was born out of wedlock."

That word again! Elizabeth turned beet red.

He faced Andrew squarely. "And, what is your role in this? Are you the father?"

"No, sir. The child's mother and I have recently been married."

The bishop addressed Elizabeth, "Yet, you didn't want him when he was born?"

His words singed like a hot poker. She shot back, "That isn't true! I have wanted my son since before he was born. I was very near death so I had to relinquish my rights to my parents. They made the decision, not I!"

The bishop did not seem to be ruffled by her retort.

"And, what about you, the grandparents?"

"We are in agreement with our daughter. She has married a stable man from a good family. Much different circumstances than when the baby was born. My wife and I have grieved over our mistake many times. We want Matthew as much as Elizabeth and Andrew do. We want to be a complete family."

"I see." He took some time before he continued. "If he was returned today, what arrangements could you make?"

This must have thrown Francis a curve because he cleared his throat before replying, "We have a large house in Alexandria. Andrew, Elizabeth and Matthew could live with us in their own suite of rooms, until they have other arrangements. We have a trusted maid who will help with the child, if needed."

The bishop leaned back in his chair and fiddled with a pencil.

"I am not one bit pleased that Father Joseph and the Mother Superior couldn't come to an agreement in this matter. I am much too busy a man to have to deal with custodial issues, but the responsibility has been placed with me and I wish to clear it as soon as possible."

He leaned forward in a confidential manner. "Do you realize there is a wealthy and notable Catholic couple who have been designated as his adoptive parents? They can offer the child a comfortable home, quality education and a sizeable inheritance."

Andrew sprang up from his chair. "We can offer him the love of his true mother and grandparents and an adoptive father who is not without means."

266

Andrew's heated response caused three priests to look up.

The bishop motioned to Andrew to take his seat.

"I will take all of this into consideration. I assume the grandparents will sign the papers to rescind the adoption, and then sign their rights back to the two of you."

They all nodded in agreement.

Andrew spoke, "I apologize if I was out of place."

"Quite all right, major. What if this war takes you away leaving Matthew without a father?"

"He would be in the hands of three people who love him. Life is never certain for any of us, wouldn't you agree?"

The bishop smiled but made no reply to the question. Instead, he advised, "I thank all of you for coming. I will have an answer in ten days. This meeting is concluded."

The young seminarian appeared, as if by magic. He escorted the four visitors through the big arched doors, under the oaks to the large iron gate.

"May God's peace go with you," he said.

The four of them waited on a bench for the cab to return. Their audience had lasted fifteen minutes.

"Ten days," lamented Elizabeth. "What could take him so long? He said he wanted this over and done."

"It's a serious decision," Andrew answered. "We want him to review all information. We have to hope we made a favorable impression. If he was settled on the adoptive couple, he would have already made that choice, I believe."

"He didn't give us much time," said Gertrude.

"No, but he had a huge lot of papers to plow through regarding the case. Keep in mind Jacob Cunningham said the priest is on our side, whether that has anything to do with it or not."

The tinny cab rattled up and made the return trip to the fashionable home in Alexandria.

"Father, were you serious about us moving into the house if we needed to?"

"Definitely."

"That may be an imposition we will have to accept, once we get the word Matthew is to come home."

When they returned to the house in Alexandria, Andrew and Elizabeth went to her room to spend as much time together as they could before they both had to leave: Andrew to the base and Elizabeth to the train. She lay in his arms and gave an audible sigh. "Will we ever spend time together as a normal married couple?"

"Once we get our lives together, I hope to secure quarters at the base similar to what Asa and Carolyn have. Then it will be more like a regular job, off in the morning and back in the evening."

"Or off to the war," she replied.

He tipped her chin up "What did I tell you about that? No worry about what hasn't happened."

"I forgot." She hesitated before she asked, "Do you think the bishop will favor us?"

"Elizabeth..."

"Right. No worry until we have to."

Opal rang a small crystal bell announcing lunchtime. It was noon, and Andrew had to be back for a meeting at one o'clock, while Elizabeth had to catch the two-o'clock train back to the Bluemont station.

They said a sad, hasty goodbye. All the way home on the train Elizabeth ran the events of the meeting with the bishop through her mind. Ten long agonizing days she would have to wait. Each day would be marked off as a prisoner marks off his sentence.

Chapter 28

What could Elizabeth do for ten days? Mary Lee's wedding was coming up the next Saturday. It was a Godsend.

When she wasn't busy in the hat shop, she attacked the apartment. She washed everything washable, swept and dusted every nook and cranny. She raked the yard to make it presentable for the expected wedding and fell into bed, exhausted, when evening came.

Elizabeth decided it was time to tell Mary Lee about Matthew. She had put it off as long as she could. Once Mary Lee wed she would move to the farm, and Elizabeth would join Andrew in Washington. It meant going their separate ways. It was only fair to tell her friend as she had promised she would. There may not be another chance.

When Mary Lee arrived on Wednesday, Elizabeth put the CLOSED sign in the window.

"Come sit down and have some tea before we get busy. Is your dress ready?"

"Miz' Butler said I can pick it up Friday. The minister told Robert he can load the tables and chairs that day, too."

Elizabeth cleared space on the work counter. "How are they going to get that furniture back to the church?"

"Robert's goin' to park the wagon in that lane behind yer fence. His brothers are gonna' take them back."

"Then, I think we have everything covered." Elizabeth lifted the tea cozy from the teapot and poured each a hot cup of tea before she took a seat opposite the young woman who had been her strength through this year of turmoil.

"Mary Lee, do you remember how I've said that one day we will have a long chat about the reason why I came here?"

"You don't have to tell me anythin'. It don't matter why you came here."

"I want you to know, although it may alter your opinion of me. I hope you will understand. It's not something I'm proud of, but I can't hide it under the rug any longer. Mary Lee, I have a child."

As Elizabeth expected, her friend's blue eyes opened wide and her jaw dropped. She was speechless.

Elizabeth continued with her story and it was one-half hour they sat with Elizabeth unfolding the tale.

At times Mary Lee dabbed at her eyes with a handkerchief. When the chronology of events was finished, she sat stark still. "Why, Miz' Elizabeth, that's the saddest thing I ever heard. No wonder you felt so bad when you came here."

"I hadn't fully recovered from the ordeal when my parents decided I should get away from Alexandria. I have been so ashamed; I just couldn't tell you before."

271

"There's no shame in it, although lotsa' people would make it so. Yer right to sell this hat shop and move back to where you want to be."

Elizabeth took Mary Lee's hand. "I'm not sure I could have survived without you being here."

"Once I went through that marriage to Zack, and then him gettin' killed on the train tracks an' all, I figured I could just about live through anythin'." She wiped a tear from her eye. "But havin' a baby taken away from me? I ain't so sure about that."

Elizabeth got up from her chair and put her hand on her friend's shoulder. "So, I haven't ruined your wedding day?"

"Matter of fact," said Mary Lee, blowing her nose, "I feel like we got all the trash outta' the way. I promise this is just between you and me."

"I prefer it that way. Until I get him back no one needs to know. And, I may not get him back."

"Now, you stop thinkin' that way right now," Mary Lee cautioned. "Does he look like you? I'd sure like to see him."

Elizabeth held a wistful look. "I hope that some day you will."

****

As the tealeaves predicted, Saturday turned out to be a sunny, glorious day. It must have been the fire in the church that had caused the dark cloud. The gazebo was decorated with garlands of honeysuckle, bridal wreath and lilies.

Mary Lee looked radiant in her cream colored, lace, wedding dress. Irene Butler had taken

272

special pains sewing on pearls and rhinestones in the waist and bodice and around the long cuffed lace sleeves. The headpiece Mary Lee had fashioned circled the crown of her head with organza and dried flowers setting off red hair that curled around her face in ringlets.

Elizabeth wore pink lace with a matching headpiece. Her blond hair had been cut in a shorter style of the day that accented her fine features.

Robert waited in the gazebo in a three-piece dark suit, high collared white shirt and patterned navy blue tie. As promised, his brothers also dressed in suits. It appeared they would be more comfortable wrestling cows, but they were doing a fine job of ushering guests to their seats.

Elizabeth smiled at the transformation in her backyard. The tables were laden with food placed on white tablecloths from the church, and the chairs were placed with an aisle between for the wedding party to pass through. Music from a fiddle and bass violin were entertaining those in attendance.

Sequestered in the back room of the hat shop were Elizabeth and Mary Lee. The bride-to-be was a bundle of nerves. "I'm gonna' fall down, I just know it."

"You are not going to fall down," said Elizabeth. "Here, I poured some wine earlier just in case you would need it."

"Oh my lands, no. I'd fall down fer sure with that stuff."

"Good," said Elizabeth. "I can use it." Three swallows and it was gone. The bride was not the only one with the jitters.

"Mary Lee, if I don't get a chance to say this again, I hope you are very happy. Although we may go our separate ways, promise me that we will never lose touch."

"I promise," answered Mary Lee. "We don't have to swear in blood or anythin' like the Indians do, do we?" She gave a nervous laugh.

Elizabeth squeezed her hand. "Not today. Red would clash with this pink dress, and imagine what it would look like dripping onto your cream lace. Besides, wouldn't that be the talk of the town? Jeremy Talley could put it on the front page of the *Courier*: *Wedding Turns Into a Bloody Mess*. Your day would truly be memorable."

"Yeah, right along with the church catchin' fire."

Elizabeth laughed aloud and quickly covered her mouth lest someone might hear.

"You shouldn't had that glass of wine," said Mary Lee, and they giggled like teenagers.

Elizabeth pulled the corner of the curtain aside and peeked at the gathering in the backyard. "Do you want to see who's out there?"

"I'll see soon enough. I'm so nervous I cain't sit or stand. Tell me who you see."

"Well, Jeremy Talley is sitting in the front row of chairs, while Lavinia is flitting about."

"Yeah, that sounds like Miz' Talley." Mary Lee patted perspiration from her face with a hankie.

"Then I see Lloyd Pierce coming in with Mrs. Pierce, and Dr. and Mrs. Hawthorne are sitting in the third row next to Irene Butler."

Elizabeth dropped the corner of the curtain. "Listen."

They heard *Here Comes the Bride* on the fiddle and bass violin. They straightened immediately.

Elizabeth grabbed up two bouquets of flowers and thrust the one with white roses at Mary Lee. "Here's your bouquet. Try not to shake too much. You don't want your petals falling off. Are you ready?"

Mary Lee cast her eyes toward heaven. "Please Lord, help me make it to that gazebo."

****

After the ceremony was over and Robert and Mary Lee drove away in the loaned two-seat carriage, Robert's brothers loaded up the wagon, parked behind the fence, with borrowed tables, chairs and tablecloths. They were off to deliver then to the Presbyterian Church.

Elizabeth was pleased with the affair and glad that it had been a special day for her friend. She only had to get through one more lonely night before she returned to Washington.

Chapter 29

Elizabeth was on the earliest train headed for Washington on Sunday morning. Monday would be the tenth day and she wanted to be there when the call came announcing the bishop's decision regarding the fate of Matthew. She missed Andrew desperately.

Taking the trolley from the station, she arrived at her parents' house in the early afternoon. Opal greeted her at the door. Gertrude and Francis Fairchilds sat in the parlor where Francis was reading the Sunday *Post* and his wife was engrossed in a knitting project. They looked up when Elizabeth entered.

Francis greeted her. "I could have picked you up at the station."

Elizabeth kissed them both. "I know, Father, but it was easy to get the trolley. "Have you heard from Andrew?"

Her mother answered, "He called an hour ago to say he'll be here around seven but he has to leave early in the morning."

It wasn't the news she wanted to hear. "If he has to be off early, he won't be here when we get word of the bishop's decision."

"Perhaps not, but at least you will get to see him," came her mother's slight admonishment.

Elizabeth took a seat and tried to settle in. The room was quiet except for the clicking of the knitting needles and rattling of the paper as pages were turned. She leafed through a magazine, rifled through a book, twiddled the necklace she wore and finally said, "I'm going out for a walk."

"Good idea," agreed her father. "You're jumpy as a cat."

"I can't help it, I'm just twisted up in knots about tomorrow."

"That's understandable, but we must wait. It isn't going to help to work yourself into a lather," came her father's sensible reply.

Elizabeth walked toward the door and called over her shoulder, "I'll be back around six."

Her mother looked up from her knitting. "You should stay here. What shall we tell Andrew, if he arrives early?"

"Tell him I'll be back at six. I have to get some air."

"Then go ahead," encouraged her father.

****

Andrew didn't arrive early It was almost seven-thirty before he rang the doorbell of the Fairchilds' residence. Elizabeth was upstairs in their room when she heard the bell and came running down the stairs. She flung open the door and fell into his arms.

He dropped the bag he carried and kissed her soundly. "Well this is more than I expected."

She threw both arms around his neck. "I have missed you so much."

277

"It couldn't be any more than I've missed you," he answered and kissed her once again.

The Fairchilds arrived on the scene. The men shook hands, and Andrew kissed his mother-in-law on the cheek.

"Sorry I'm later than I'd hoped."

"You're here and that's what counts," said Francis.

Gertrude chimed in, "I had Opal wait dinner for you two. I assumed you would be hungry."

"That was kind of you. I'm starved. I didn't get a chance to eat before I left the base."

"I'm sure this war business has turned everything upside down. Mother and I are retiring for the evening so you two can have some time to yourselves." Francis guided his wife toward their room at the back of the house.

They bid the parents goodnight before going into the kitchen to dig into the dinner Opal had prepared.

"As soon as we're finished, Andrew, let's hop into bed. I have so much to tell you."

"I agree with the hopping into bed, but I'm not sure when we will get to the conversation part of it."

She shook her head. "Tsk, tsk, tsk."

****

The next morning Andrew was up at five o'clock. He slipped out of bed without disturbing Elizabeth and dressed quietly. He smiled down at his sleeping wife. Her peaceful countenance gave him hope for the day ahead.

They had talked until midnight. Elizabeth did have a lot to report. She had described Mary Lee's wedding and all the hullabaloo surrounding it. How easily Mary Lee had accepted the news of Matthew, and saving the best news of all that she had put the hat shop up for sale.

Andrew had done his best to lend a polite ear.

Having to leave so early was an irritation. He wanted to be here when they got the bishop's answer.

That wasn't all that was causing him aggravation. Being on General Pershing's staff allowed him to get information before it was made public. Not only would today bring a decision regarding Matthew but it would also be the day when the military would begin to conscript soldiers. 17,000 men would be deployed to the war in Europe sometime during the month.

If he is sent off to war and Matthew isn't returned, he was concerned that it may prove to be too much for Elizabeth. Although she had proved to have strength, there is only so much a person can bear. He had been the one to push her into marriage for his own selfishness. He was the one who advised her not to worry about what hasn't happened; why couldn't he take his own advice?

She slept so peacefully he dared not kiss her before he left. So, he opened the door, quietly went down the stairs and out the back door of the house.

****

It was close to ten o'clock when Elizabeth came into the kitchen.

"Land sakes, child. You must have been one tired girl."

"Good morning, Opal. I hope you have some breakfast ready. I'm starved. When did Andrew leave?" She picked up a biscuit and put some jam on it.

"Afore I came. I got some hot coffee on the stove if you want a cup."

"That should wake me up. I can't imagine why I was so tired."

Opal smiled at her as she brought the coffee to the table. "I 'spect it's 'cause most of the worry has gone out of you. How about a couple eggs?"

"And, bacon?" added Elizabeth.

"You just sit here and enjoy your coffee while I slice off a couple pieces and fry you up some eggs."

It must have been the smell of the bacon frying that brought Gertrude Fairchilds into the room. "It's almost lunchtime, Elizabeth. I can't believe you could sleep this long, especially on such an important day."

"Does Father have any idea when we will hear from the lawyer?"

"Not even a guess," said her mother taking a seat opposite her daughter. She looked around the room as if she were seeing the kitchen for the first time. "We always eat in the dining room. I don't think I've ever eaten in here," she observed.

Opal smiled to herself as she worked around the stove. The whole atmosphere in the house had taken a change. "Can I pour you a cup of coffee, ma'am?" she asked Gertrude.

"You can fry me up some eggs and bacon while you're at it." They all laughed.

"Have you had any offers on your shop, Elizabeth?"

"I think it's too soon. I expect the banker will bring someone by, if he has an interested buyer."

"I suppose so. I assume the wedding went off without any major hitches."

"That it did. I planned most of it. Robert wanted it to be a memorable affair and I can say that it was."

"And, you and that little girl are still close friends?" Gertrude raised her eyebrows.

"We are. I know we have opposite backgrounds, but she was the reason I didn't collapse."

Her mother shook her head." I'm sure there were other young ladies of your stature that would have befriended you."

"Well, I'm not going to discuss it. Mary Lee knows how to keep a confidence and her deep feelings are sincere. What more can you ask for in a true friend?"

Francis Fairchilds came into the kitchen. "It's noisy in here."

"Well, yes," said Gertrude, "with the bacon frying, and the copper washing machine thumping away in the back room. Elizabeth and I have been having a conversation."

"So have I. Jacob Cunningham called. We are to be in his office at two o'clock this afternoon."

Elizabeth jumped up from her chair. "What did the bishop say?"

"Jacob doesn't have that information yet. Apparently, we are to meet with him and that priest, Father Joseph."

Gertrude sighed, "Have some bacon and eggs, Francis," advised his wife. "It looks like this is going to be our lunch."

****

Francis backed his Ford tin-lizzie out of the garage. Gertrude wore an outdated ankle-length brocade dress and large leghorn hat. Elizabeth was dressed demurely in a navy blue calf-length suit and wore a simple hat to match. It took them almost an hour to get to Jacob's office. Elizabeth thought it would have been faster to take the trolley, but her father said the reason he bought a car was to bypass the trolley fares. They jostled through the city of Washington at a slow pace.

The anxious trio: Francis, Gertrude and Elizabeth were seated in Jacob Cunningham's office waiting for the priest.

Father Joseph was fifteen minutes late. "It's a buggar trying to get across this city, anymore." They sat around a table in a room adjacent to Jacob's office.

The priest had just removed papers from his valise when the secretary opened the door announcing, "Major Caldwell."

Elizabeth drew in a loud breath. Andrew reached for her hand as he took the seat next to her.

"Glad you could make it, Major," said Jacob. "I guess Father Joseph's delay was a hidden blessing."

"Mr. Cunningham, it appears you have influence with my superiors. I am most appreciative," acknowledged Andrew.

"If we are ready, let's get this matter settled," encouraged the priest.

They all nodded.

"The bishop wishes me to express that this has been a difficult decision for him. He also wishes me to tell you that he has talked with the Mother Superior and the potential adoptive parents. His role in the outcome for Matthew Quinton Fairchilds is not to be taken lightly. Therefore, he sent me as his messenger, to tell you that after giving careful thought and careful review of all facets of this case," he paused and looked directly at Elizabeth, "he is in favor of rescinding the adoption…"

"Oh thank God!" shouted Elizabeth, and they all burst out with joyous applause.

The priest raised his hand to quell their enthusiasm. "There is one stipulation for the child's return. If you are unwilling to fulfill this requirement, the bishop will let the adoption process proceed."

Andrew spoke up, "And, that is?"

Father Joseph cleared his throat and peered over his glasses. "The child will be raised Roman Catholic."

"This is unbelievable!" Francis erupted. "We're Episcopalians!"

Elizabeth jumped up from her seat. "Of course we will raise him Roman Catholic," she cried. "If it hadn't been for Father Quinn in Winchester and Sister Mary Claire, I would never have found my child or known his fate. I promise that he will be raised in the Catholic faith." She turned to her father. "This is no time for petty differences!"

Father Joseph raised his eyebrows before addressing Andrew, "And, what of you, sir?"

"I believe his mother has spoken for both of us."

Elizabeth sat down and slipped her arm through Andrew's.

"There are two more requirements."

The four sat upright and leaned forward with apprehension written on their faces. The priest continued, "The grandparents must sign their rights back to Mrs. Caldwell, and Major Caldwell must sign as the adoptive father. Are we all in agreement?"

All voiced agreement except for Francis who was still reeling from the fact that he would have a Roman Catholic grandchild. Gertrude poked him in the ribs with her elbow and he gave a startled nod.

"His name will be Matthew Andrew Caldwell," announced Elizabeth giving a tentative look to Andrew. A quick squeeze of her hand and silent wide grin showed his pleased acceptance.

Jacob Cunningham was all smiles. "I am happy for all of you. After a couple of changes in the wording, we will get these papers signed so they can get to the courthouse as soon as possible."

Elizabeth turned to Father Joseph. "When can Matthew come to us?"

"How soon will you be prepared to bring him home?"

Gertrude answered, "As soon as possible." She turned to Elizabeth. "I have everything ready. Opal and I went up to the attic and cleaned up the crib and highchair and the wicker carriage. I have bought new sheets and nightclothes and have them stored in the bureau in the guest room. I was hesitant to tell you before we knew if Matthew would be coming home."

Elizabeth leaned forward and touched her mother's hand before addressing the priest, "Please tell the bishop that we are most grateful to him. We will give Matthew the home and love he deserves."

All signatures were in place and Father Joseph was tucking the papers into his valise when he casually mentioned, "The bishop also said we may have lost an added wing to the hospital in this process." He offered a sly smile. "You may pick up your child at St. Anthony's Home whenever you are ready, Mrs. Caldwell. Now, I must fight my way back across this city. May God bless you all."

Elizabeth seemed to be in a daze.

Andrew stood at her side and took charge. "Francis, you take Mother Fairchilds on home. Elizabeth and I will take a taxi to St. Anthony's."

"Right you are," replied Francis. "We'll have the child's room ready and waiting." He shook Jacob's hand. "We can't thank you enough for all you've done."

The pleased lawyer smiled, "As I said before, your bill will be in the mail."

****

It was six o'clock when Andrew and Elizabeth arrived at the large house in Alexandria. They had spent over an hour at the orphanage getting acquainted with Matthew. He had had so many different caretakers over the year that he showed little hesitation warming up to both of his new parents. Once he was allowed to bring his favorite blanket with him, he showed no signs of discontent and was happily resting in Andrew's arm as they came up the walk. Elizabeth's arm was linked through her husband's. The cares of the future tucked away.

The proud grandparents and Opal stood in the open doorway of the welcoming house in Alexandria with joy written on their faces as they surveyed the young family coming up the walk: Andrew, the stately son-in-law whose understanding and love knew no limits; Elizabeth, the fair-haired daughter whose courage and strength blossomed in the search for her son; and, Matthew, the beautiful child who brought them all together.

About the Author

Millie Curtis, a native of Oneida, New York, has made her home in the Shenandoah Valley of Virginia since 1975. After a career in nursing and raising a family, she is pleased to have the time to write and perhaps bring smiles and pleasurable moments to those who read her works. There are few troubles that an hour's worth of reading will not dissipate.

Other novels by Millie Curtis:

Beyond the Red Gate
The Milliner

CPSIA information can be obtained at www.ICGtesting.com
Printed in the USA
BVOW041133060613

322631BV00001B/1/P